In the Shadow of a Vow

Novella 4.1

Scarlett & Tomas

By Maci Aurora

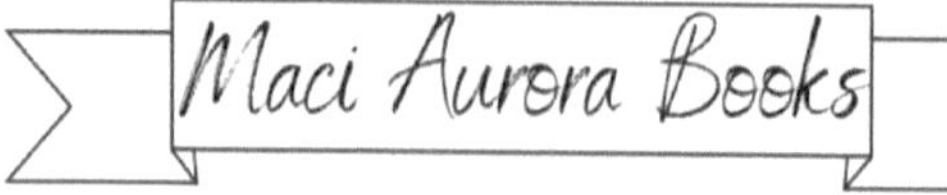

In the Shadow of a Wish, book 1
In the Shadow of a Hoax, book 2
In the Shadow of a Dream, book 3
In the Shadow of the Truth—the Novellas, Book 4
In the Shadow of a Vow, book 4.1

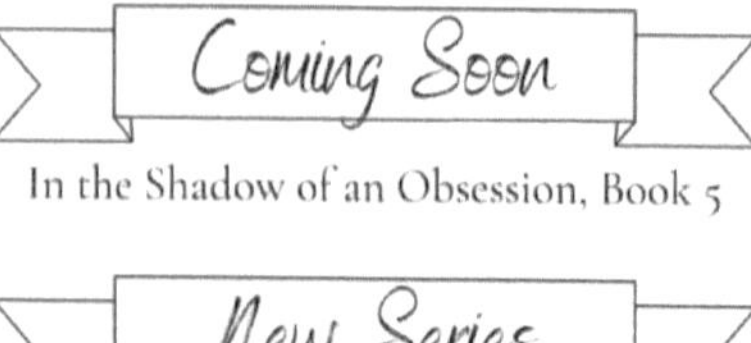

In the Shadow of an Obsession, Book 5

The Accidental Seraph, Carran Hollow Fated-Mates book 1

The Ring Academy: The Trials of Imogene Sol

The Messy Truth About Love

The Stories Stars Tell
In the Echo of this Ghost Town
When the Echo Answers

The Letters She Left Behind

In the Shadow of a Vow

A Fareview Fairytale Novella

Book 4.1

By Maci Aurora

In the Shadow of a Vow
Fareview Fairytale Book 4.1
©2024 Maci Aurora w/ Mixed Plate Press
Honolulu, Hawaii

cover art: Sara Oliver Designs

ISBN: 979-8-9891543-9-5 (paperback)
ISBN: 979-8-9891543-4-0 (eBook)

About this book: *In the Shadow of a Vow* was inspired by a mash up of Grimm's Fairytales, "The Princess in Disguise," "Tom Thumb," "The Robber Bridegroom," and "Maid Maleen." It contains explicit sexual situations and is intended for mature audiences (18+).

DEDICATED TO

My husband.

Scarlett

Scarlett Fareview, mother to Jessamine, Tarley, Brinna, Aurielle, and Mattias, wife to Tomas, and runaway daughter to the Mad King Zollah Cumbria and Queen Alea Cumbria of Echo Landing, had failed. Sitting near the fire with a blanket wrapped around her shoulders, she watched as others in the cottage spoke, could hear their voices, but nothing coherent penetrated the haze that consumed her.

Her second born, Tarley, wrapped up in her husband Lachlan's embrace, stared unseeing. Brinna, third in the order of her children, had her hand in Auri's, her fourth. The youngest, Mattias, stood, his arms across his chest, looking like the man he'd become while they'd been sleeping, talking to the gods, Nixus and his brother, Lucian a few paces away.

And Jessamine, her first born was missing.

A sob ripped through Scarlett's throat, and she caught the sound with her hand pressed against her mouth.

She'd failed.

She looked for her constant companion—the love of her life—and found him staring unseeing into the fire across from her. Tears filled her eyes, and his form blurred. She shouldn't cry, knew she didn't deserve the pity rising in her heart like a raging sea, but the flood came anyway.

"I'm sorry," she whispered. "I thought–"

Tomas turned his head, his forest eyes finding hers—but for the first time since she'd know him, they were empty, as if his soul had been scooped out and discarded. He didn't smile. He'd always been the one to smile, no matter the circumstances. He was the one who saw the world in rose, painted any situation with positivity.

Now, he looked at her with hollow eyes, opening his mouth to say something but didn't, turning back to the fire once more.

Her heart cracked open, leaking out the substance that made her who she was.

A commotion at the door grabbed her attention, along with everyone else in the cottage.

"Your highness." A soldier stood in the doorway. He was tall and lean, his face pressed from granite. His features were sharp, his green eyes bright and his wheat hair short.

On his chest, he wore the leather breastplate stamped with the tree of Jast, a short sword strapped to his back.

Tarley's husband, the Crown Prince of Jast, stepped forward. "Jude."

The man ducked his head in deference.

It reminded Scarlett of a life before. Before her mother had died. The irony wasn't lost to Scarlett. No one knew her children were of royal blood, and they were also godblood descended from gods on her mother's side. She'd concealed those facts to hide them, but now that was over.

Jessamine was missing.

Scarlett knew who had her daughter, but how to find him was another matter. She didn't even know where to begin. The witch in the woods, perhaps, but the last time they had met, when Scarlett had insisted on the sleeping spell in spite of the witch's wisdom to forge a different path, the witch had said it was the last time they would speak.

"Where?" Lachlan said, his tone loud enough to capture Scarlett's attention once more.

"He left," the soldier named Jude said, looking over his shoulder, then back.

"Johesha left? His post?"

"He handed me this" –Jude handed whatever it was to Lachlan– "and said he'd be back."

Lachlan frowned. "I don't understand."

"There was someone in the hedge when it...

disappeared," Jude said.

Scarlett stood, her heart thumping painfully.

"The stranger was carrying... someone, and Johesha said he was going after her."

"Jessamine," Scarlett said and every face in the room swiveled to her. "He has Jessamine."

Emotions flashed across their faces: anger, frustration, hurt, dismissal. She couldn't blame them. She'd known this would be the case, even if her intentions had been to protect them.

She'd failed.

Baba told you it was a house built of cards.

"*He* who?" Mattias shouted. "Tell the truth. I'm fucking sick of your lies."

He was seething, shocking Scarlett. Her son, who'd always been like his father, was genial and slow to anger, but the rage in his eyes was like a living creature, breathing fire.

Scarlett looked down at the floor.

"Mattias," Tomas said, his voice a warning.

"She drugged us," Auri snapped. "She deserves our anger, Father."

Tomas didn't argue. Frankly, neither could Scarlett.

"Who is *he*?" Mattias asked.

The layers of spells had been broken. There were no ribbons, no hedge, no sleeping spell. Scarlett stood before her family and their loved ones completely exposed for the first time in the 28 years since she and Tomas had disappeared behind the hedge.

Now, with nothing to hide behind, no spell to determine what she shared, there was no reason to conceal the truth any longer but for the pain it would cause her to relive it.

"I don't know his true name," she said, turning back to her children.

Jessamine was missing.

"True name?"

"Your given name. Like mine–" But her throat closed around the words, and she wished Tomas was standing beside her, giving her strength.

But he had been, hadn't he. The entire time. He'd been the strong one all along and she'd failed to listen to him, failed to honor his strength and belief in her. Failed to trust his wisdom.

She tried again to say her true name, but she hadn't uttered those sounds for a lifetime, had tried to forget they existed. Her true name was attached to a promise stripped away by pain and prevarication.

"Wait. It's not–" Tarley frowned.

"Your name is Scarlett," Auri said.

Brinna—her dreamer—was silent, but Scarlett noticed when her daughter's gaze sought the golden god's.

Swallowing the sounds that cut like glass, she sighed,

dug deeper for her own strength, and finally uttered the curse. "Azleah. My real name."

Brinna, sweet Brinna, burst into tears and turned into the golden god's—Lucian's—arms.

Scarlett didn't understand Brianna's reaction.

Lucian's gaze rose to meet Scarlett's. She wasn't sure how to decipher his look, but she felt supported somehow.

"But why?" Auri sank to the bench near the table. Alone.

Scarlett's eyes jumped to Nixus, the dark god, waiting for him to move to Auri's side. They'd expressed their intention to exchange vows with one another, but he remained where he was, his eyes on her daughter, but changed, somehow removed. This wasn't how they'd been, before...

Something was wrong.

Scarlett sank back into her chair. "It's time I tell you the story." She paused as the words stuck like broken glass in her throat once more. "But it isn't an easy story to hear," she said, spitting them out as her chin quivered. "I know it's past time you knew it."

Then she began...

Once upon a time . . .

Azleah Cumbria, first and only daughter of Zollah Cumbria, king of Echo Landing, and his late wife, Alea, knelt at the death mound of her mother. She'd visited nearly every day for the last three years, since her mother's untimely passing, if only to find comfort in what once was rather than what it had become since her mother had returned to the stars.

The steep peaks of the mountains tipped with snow rose around them in the valley of the dead. Mounds much like her mother's, a testament to the royal Cumbria line, dotted the landscape, though her mother's was the most recent. The white blossoms of the lox heather covered the mound, and for that Azleah was grateful. Something beautiful to give her a moment of peace and hope. Moisture seeped through the fabric of her wool dress as a stiff wind whipped at her braid, grabbing hold of her red tresses and pulling them from the plait. Both reminded her that peace was temporary.

"Mistress?" her companion said quietly from behind her, though Azleah could hear the distress in Nettle's tone.

Azleah didn't answer, offering a prayer instead to the gods that they might take mercy on her. "Please," she whispered. "Mother. He's not himself anymore. I don't know what to do."

But the gods remained silent.

"They're coming!" Nettle's fear rang out in her whispered warning.

Nettle's hand slid into Azleah's, her grip tight, but still Azleah didn't move. She held her friend's hand, head bowed, and continued to beg the gods for their mercy, hoping that at her mother's graveside somehow, she would be saved. That maybe her estranged grandparents—gods of fabled Elysian—might even hear her prayer.

Still she prayed, even as the sound of heavy footsteps in the sod surrounded them. It wasn't until she heard Hale Commander Arn's "Princess" that she looked up.

She'd considered running, but there wasn't anywhere to go. There wasn't a soul in this godsforsaken kingdom that would harbor her from the mad king. The palace guard—seven of them—surrounded her and Nettle, an enclosed circle around the girls and the mound of her mother's bones. Each man stood at attention in their royal regalia—leather and buckles, bracers and breastplates, swords and daggers—waiting for the order to seize her. It wouldn't matter where she ran. They would find her.

Azleah stood, Nettle's hand still in hers. She straightened her spine and lifted her chin, looking at Hale Commander Arn. "You know this is wrong," she said, feeling so much older than her sixteen years.

"He's my king."

"And he is not right. Not since–" Her eyes slid to the grave. Nothing had been right since her mother had died. "You know this."

"I made a vow." Hale Arn's eyes slid away, dragging guilt with them.

"To uphold the honor of the throne," she said. "There's no honor in this."

He didn't respond, didn't look at her, his gaze elsewhere.

Nettle's grip tightened. "He's coming," she whispered.

Azleah looked from the Hale Commander's pale face and followed Nettle's gaze to watch her father walk through the swaying grass toward her, framed by the massive stone castle behind him. He was dressed strangely in the thick, full-length fur robes layered with chains of gold he'd taken to wearing, uncharacteristic of the man she'd once known. His hair, which had been a dark brown threaded with copper, had turned white over the last three years. It was too long over his shoulders and in need of washing. His beard was scraggly and drooped down his chest. The worst change, she knew, would be the moment she met his gaze. His once deep gray eyes had changed color, now a disconcerting blue blasted with striations of red and rimmed with a ring of bright copper. He had the manic twitch of a man invested in too many mind-altering petals.

Nettle dropped to her knees, and the soldiers of the guard dropped their gazes.

Azleah remained where she was, the wind whipping her dark blue dress around her legs.

"Lord Father," she greeted him, dipping her chin to her chest in acknowledgement of his place as king for just a moment before looking up, hopeful he'd changed his mind.

That something, anything, a miracle had intervened on her behalf. That the crazed look would suddenly be cleared from his vision.

The Mad King stopped an arm's length away, his awful witch—the horrible reason for his dabbling in necromancy—several steps behind him. Her father had once been called Zollah the Benevolent with Azleah's mother at his side. While Azleah understood the stripping effects of grief, it had broken and torn away who he'd once been and had formed him into what he'd become: a man succumbed to the darkness of malignant magic, leaching anything that was once good from him.

"Alea." He dipped his head, the crown of bones looking like spikes in his white hair.

"I'm Azleah," she said. "Your daughter." Her hand drifted out, gesturing to the grave mound. "Mother is there."

He didn't look, his awful eyes fixed on her, and instead took another step closer. "You're returning to me," he said and smiled. He reached out and slid a finger over her cheek.

Tears filled Azleah's eyes. Memories of the father she loved stayed with her. When she was little, when Mother had still been alive, he'd been everything a father should be: kind, protective, patient. He'd held her hand as they'd walked through the gardens. He'd taught her to swim when they'd visited the sea. He'd read her stories and patiently waited with a smile on his handsome face while she told him her own stories. He'd offered wisdom when she'd been frustrated and hugs when she'd been hurt. He'd loved her and her mother with absolute conviction.

This man, filled with grief and rage and dark magic, wasn't the man she'd known. Not anymore.

Not only had she lost her mother, but her father as well.

She couldn't contain her sob, stifling it with her hand

before pleading, "Father. Please. I'm not Mother." She turned her head and looked at the guards. "Please," she begged. "Help me."

But instead of intervening, their gazes drifted away.

Her father's worshipful gaze jumped from her to look at each of the guards with accusation and mistrust. "They want you for themselves." The words dripped from his tongue with malice. "They want to steal you away from me." He snatched her hand and yanked her after him as he stalked back over the grassy plateau of Remembrance Valley toward the castle. "This is for the best."

"No." She pulled, but he adjusted his grip, reeling her closer.

Nettle kept hold of Azleah's other hand and jerked to her feet, following behind.

"Alea, your reincarnation isn't complete," he rambled. "The witch says I must keep you safe until then. Keep you from someone who might want to steal you away from me."

"Father!" she screamed. "Stop!"

"Then we'll marry. And everything will return to how it was."

"Stop, Father. Stop!"

But he didn't listen, dragging her through the wooden door of the palace. He drew her through the hallways, servants dropping to their knees as they passed. Their eyes lifted to watch the procession, to listen to his ramblings and her begging through her tears, their heads following as they passed. No one intervened. The guards had fallen in behind them, their quick steps smacking against the stone.

"The tower is the safest," the king was saying. "Witch and I have made it safe. You'll see. And then when we marry—when your change is complete—all will be well. I promise."

"Father!" She fought his hold, but his physical strength was uncompromising even if his mental capacity had faded. "I'm not her. She's gone. Dead. Mother hasn't come back."

Her pleas fell on uncompromising ears.

When they reached the new tower door, Azleah fought, jerking backward.

Her father's grip tightened. "Witch said you would fight, but it is only because you don't understand what's happening to you. You're lost in the remaking," he said. "Trust me."

Nettle's grip slipped from Azleah's.

Azleah turned her head, frantically searching for her companion. "Nettle? Nettle! Don't leave me!"

But the guards restrained her best friend, her only companion. Though Nettle fought through tears and protests, she wasn't a match.

The king forced Azleah, fighting and screaming, through the arched doorway into an alcove at the base of a set of spiral stairs. Still, she fought, her nails breaking against the stone, the wood, but it was useless.

"Two more years," her father said. "Then you'll be yourself, and we can be together."

He shut the door between them, and the sound of a key sliding into the mechanism clicked. Final.

A dark gold light flashed over the wooden door before blinking out and trapping Azleah inside.

From beyond, she could hear Nettle's cries matching her own, fading as she was taken away.

Pressing her palms to the door, the warmth of its magic leaching into her skin, Azleah leaned her forehead against the wood, then drew back and pounded it with her fists. "Let me out," she cried, then shrieked. "Let me out!"

Over and over she called until she was hoarse from screaming, until there was no sound on the other side of the door but the echo of her cries matching the echo in her heart.

Time passed, and Azleah was alone. The days stretched into weeks, into months, toward a year, broken only by the rising and setting sun. Though her father, in his madness, had constructed the tower room to offer comfort and diversions, Azleah struggled between the bed and a single chair that faced the small window barely bigger than her head, too small to crawl out and face a death she would have welcomed over her proposed future as the bride of her own father. She'd considered it but didn't have the means. The tower's enchantments prevented it.

She was permitted two visitors: a single lady's maid, who came each morning, and her father's trusted witch, who visited in the evening. Azleah trusted neither woman and so spoke little, sure that whatever she might say would be reported to her father.

The maid, whose name Azleah hadn't even been given, said nothing and took great care never to meet Azleah's eyes. Every morning, she climbed the stairs with Azleah's breakfast and announced like clockwork, "Your bath has been drawn, Princess." Azleah would descend the stairs for the bath awaiting her in the alcove by the locked door, and while she bathed the maid replaced her soiled clothing and bedding with clean linens. Then Azleah would climb the spiral stairs back up into the tower, and once back in her prison, the maid left.

The witch would arrive every evening, bringing Azleah dinner, but unlike the maid, the witch lingered, talking and telling her about the kingdom. "The festival in the village burned your father in effigy," she'd said one day, or "I can empathize with your plight, my dear." While Azleah was curious about what was happening in her kingdom, she had very little inclination to engage with her father's witch and only spoke to her once that first year.

"How is Nettle?" she'd asked early in her confinement. She'd been staring out that single window as the sun set casting the landscape beyond in golden relief.

"What is a Nettle?" the witch had asked.

At that, Azleah had turned her head and truly looked at

the witch for the first time. The woman was tall and thin, and while she wouldn't be called beautiful, her appearance wasn't hideous as Azleah had assumed, her features sharp and angular. Her dark hair was thick and full, reaching down her back and drawn away from her face by a sparkling fastener. She wore a dark robe over her clothes and sat in one of the chairs at the table where she set Azleah's dinner each evening.

Azleah turned back to the window. "My best friend."

The witch made a noise that stretched out from her nose, and that was all that had been said.

The next evening, the witch returned with Azleah's meal. "Hale Crue—your guard—says your Nettle has fled the palace. Not much of a best friend."

Azleah, staring out the window, didn't flinch at the news, hopeful it was true rather than a lie hiding that Nettle was dead.

More time passed, and Azleah was alone. The days continued to march on, broken only by the rising and setting sun. When Azleah opened her eyes the first morning of her seventeenth year, she cried. She was one year closer to the impending doom of her eighteenth, when she would walk from the tower dressed as a bride to marry her father.

Days passed, and Azleah stopped eating.

The witch became more insistent.

"Why aren't you eating? Your breakfast tray is full when

I retrieve it, and the maid has reported removing your dinner with most of the food still on the tray."

Azleah ignored her, as usual.

"You won't be able to fight."

It was a ludicrous statement. Azleah scoffed, wondering what it was the witch suggested she fight. Her father? His guards? Her? The damn witch was his agent.

"So you do hear me," the witch said. "What do you lose by speaking with me?"

When Azleah remained silent, the witch sighed, stood, and walked across the room to where Azleah sat. Standing next to her, the witch slid a rolled bit of parchment into Azleah's line of sight. The small roll stood out against the dark stone of the tower. It was tied together with a tiny thread of twine.

Azleah refused to give anything to the witch. Not a look, not a flinch, not a word or a sound, even though the tap of the witch's sharp, dark nails against the roll seemed to suggest she wanted one.

When Azleah didn't move, the witch finally said, "Eating will keep your strength up."

"Have you poisoned it?"

"Why would I do that? I need you alive."

"Maybe it would be a mercy," Azleah said and looked up into the witch's shrewd face.

"But that wouldn't serve the right purpose," the witch

said and leaned down to meet Azleah's gaze. Her eyes were as dark as the rest of her. "It's your kingdom, too." Then the witch left the room.

Azleah listened to the witch's steps retreat down the spiral stairs, waited for the sound of the door, then reached for the parchment. She pulled off the string, unrolled it, and read the handwritten words:

His mind is lost. It's time to get you out.

She didn't want the hope that unfurled in her chest and looked over her shoulder at the empty doorway to the stairwell.

Still, hope fluttered with curiosity and possibility. Was the witch offering her help? Azleah stood and walked to the table where her dinner waited. She looked at it, smelled it, then sat and ate.

The next day passed the same but brought with it a new note:

The people are with you.

Azleah ate her dinner and walked the stairs an extra time. She stood at the doorway, listening. "Hello?" she said.

Silence answered, but then there was a shuffle of feet beyond the door.

The next day brought another note:

Nettle is in Mercy Row, serving the House Bicus. She's safe.

Azleah ate her food and walked the stairs, stopping at

the door once more. "Hello?" she said.

This time, someone on the other side knocked. Azleah went to sleep with hope hot and bright inside her.

When the witch arrived the next day, Azleah wasn't sitting at the window, she was facing the door, waiting. She watched the witch hesitate upon entering the room, then walk to the table with Azleah's dinner. Instead of sitting as she usually did, the witch faced her. "You look better."

"Who is writing the notes you're delivering?"

The witch looked over her shoulder, a hesitation, then turned back to Azleah. "I shouldn't say, princess."

"Why would you deliver them, then?"

The witch stepped around the table. "Because you are our hope."

"From what?"

"Him."

"Yet I've been left locked in this tower."

"There's a spell," the witch started, "on the castle. Few know, those that do aren't... able to defy your father... and the rest forget. Nettle forgot the moment she left the castle."

"You cast it."

The witch nodded.

"You can undo it."

"Not without consequences. It's better to make a way forward than attempt to remake the past."

"And why should I trust anything you tell me, Witch?

It's your fault we've descended this far into hell. It was you who took him on the dark path of necromancy."

"I only wished to ease his grief, but the path he's forged is of his own doing."

"But you've aided him."

The witch hesitated, then nodded, lowering her eyes. "I cannot change what has already been done, but I can choose a different path to modify the future. I wish to help you, and I'm the only one who can."

"Convenient. And why should I believe you?"

"Because I'm not offering out of kindness." Her dark eyes met Azleah's, and they were filled with hunger. "You have something I want."

Incredulous, Azleah looked around her prison room. "What could I possibly have that you want?"

The witch took a step away and dipped her head. "I promise to reveal it, Princess, but my divination informs me it isn't time."

"And when is it time?" Azleah shouted. "The last I checked, I have less than a year before I'm forced to be a bride for... for my father." She nearly gagged on the words. "He thinks I'm my reincarnated mother. And *that* is your fault."

The witch didn't look up, remaining where she was with her head bowed. "Allow me to prove my worth, Your

Highness, and after I do, then, and only then, will I make my request."

"And how much time do you need?"

"For you, it will feel like an eternity," the witch hedged.

Azleah laughed, but there was no joy in it. "Of course. Convenient."

"I promise you, I will prove my worth."

Azleah studied the witch. She'd waited over a year and had nothing to lose by waiting another day, a week, a month. She could only hang onto the hope coursing through her veins. And if the witch failed, freedom would mean either her death or her father's. Either way, only one of them could remain alive. So she agreed.

The witch looked up and smiled as she backed away. "First" –she looked at the food– "regain your strength." Then she turned and left the tower.

Azleah ate and did her turns on the stairs, stopping at the door each time to call out, "Hello?" On the third turn, she asked, "Hello? Is anyone there?"

"Princess?" a man's voice asked from the other side of the door.

"Who are you?"

"Hale Crue," the voice replied, and Azleah recalled the name of the guard the witch had mentioned. "Your Highness, are you unwell? Do you need help? I cannot open the door."

"I am as good as can be expected, I suppose, and that is alright. Hearing another voice is nice," she said.

"Would you like to... talk?"

"I would."

"I can do that."

Azleah smiled from her side of the door. She wondered what he looked like and imagined him with dark hair and green eyes. Was he tall?

"Did the witch give you my message?" he asked.

Azleah tilted her head, looking at the grain of the door with the sheen of the spell cast over it. "You gave me a message?"

"Yes, Your Highness. I found Lady Nettle for you. She is safe."

"Oh. That was you?" She smiled and pressed her finger to a knot in the wooden door. "Yes. I received it. Thank you for giving me that peace."

"It is my duty."

She wanted to tell him to let her out—that was his duty—but knew it was futile. Between the spells and the magic lock, she wasn't sure why he needed to be out there anyway. "How do you remember it's me? The witch said–"

"I am one of the few who remember."

"Is there no way to get me out?"

"I'm afraid not, but should there ever be a moment when I can storm the tower and bring you to safety, you have my word, Princess, I will do it."

Azleah's heart trembled in her chest at his words and the vehemence with which he conveyed them. "Thank you, Hale Crue." She pressed a hand to the door.

"Don't thank me. I was there the day you were locked in," he said quietly, then fell silent on the other side of the door.

Silence descended on her side as well, shocked as she was by his admission.

"Are you still there?" he asked.

She reached for indignation and anger, but it didn't surge. Instead, she sighed, resigned to the circumstances that had victimized them all. "Yes. And there wasn't anything you could have done. Not alone."

"I wish that wasn't so, but I carry this guilt because I didn't do anything." He was silent, then, before asking, "Would you still like to talk?"

"Yes," she answered. "I would like that very much."

She slid down to the stone floor and sat with her back against the door as she and Hale Crue spoke well into the night. She learned he'd been in the palace guard since he turned sixteen, and now he was twenty-one. That to join, he'd had to leave his family and forsake them for the crown. That he wasn't allowed to marry as a palace guard, but when he was ready, he could be reassigned to the city guard ranks.

"Is there a special someone?" she'd asked.

"No, Your Highness," he'd answered. "There is no one."

All the next day, Azleah replayed the conversation in her head. When the witch arrived with her dinner, she delivered another note with her meal. The witch didn't speak but offered Azleah a slight smile and a nod before leaving.

As soon as the witch was done, Azleah tore open the message:

Dear Princess,

Thank you for speaking with me last night. I know it is too forward to speak of such things, especially considering the vast chasm between our circumstances, but I found myself hopeful and my mind replaying our conversation. Is it too much to look forward to speaking with you again?

Hale Crue

Azleah's heart kicked up the strongest rhythm she'd felt in her breast in a long time, and she was unable to keep the smile from her face.

That night, she knocked on the door. "Hale Crue?"

"Your Highness," he answered.

She could hear his smile.

There was timidity between them initially, but eventually, as midnight approached, they fell into a familiar rhythm of conversation.

And so it went, night after night. Day after day. The maid. The Witch and her messages. Conversations with her guard, Crue.

"What would you do?" Crue asked after weeks of speaking with one another. "If you could get out?"

"Claim my kingdom," she said.

"And your father?"

She didn't say she would kill him—couldn't bring herself to admit it, for some reason—so she said, "He would be treated justly. But I can't do it without supporters."

Crue was quiet for some time.

"Are you still there?" she asked.

"I will get them." His voice was barely perceptible from the other side of the door. "Supporters."

"How?" she asked. "The witch said there's a spell."

"We need to break it, then."

"It can't be done. Not without the witch."

"Then you need to do everything you can to get her to do your bidding, Your Highness."

Azleah knew he was right. It was time to demand answers.

Azleah

"I want answers, Witch," Azleah demanded the following night. After speaking with Crue, she'd spent the day ruminating on her circumstances. Despite everything stacked against her, she needed to take charge somehow. She refused to wait for the Mad King to determine her fate.

The witch hesitated at the opening to the stairwell, obviously surprised by Azleah's greeting, then regained her composure. "What sorts of answers?" She slid the tray across the round table. "There are many questions."

Azleah descended from the dais where her bed was located to where the witch stood at the tableside. "You are playing a game, somehow–"

"No game." The witch set down a rolled parchment message.

Azleah's gaze jumped to the message, greedy for it. The witch noticed, her eyes glittering with an unfamiliar gleam. Azleah didn't trust the witch, but she also knew the witch was her only way out. "What is it you want?"

The witch pulled a chair and sat. "The bones determined today isn't the day to tell you. You don't trust me yet."

"I will never trust you."

"And that will never modify the future." The witch plucked at something on the sleeve of her dark dress. "Allow me to offer a gesture of goodwill and intention."

Azleah narrowed her eyes. "Goodwill? Let me out."

The witch sighed. "As I have previously said, Princess, there are spells already cast that are unable to be broken without sacrifice. Hence consulting the bones." She gestured to emphasize her words.

"Sacrifice? What kind?"

"The death kind."

"So kill him."

"You assume whose death would be required. Perhaps if you knew, you wouldn't wish it."

"The king's?"

"No. Not his, or mine." The witch's eyes revealed the truth, a look leveled upon Azleah that she couldn't hide from.

"Mine."

The witch gave a single nod. "Timing is everything. Ask for something else."

Besides being released, there was only one thing she could think to want that was within the witch's power. "Allow Hale Crue into the tower."

The witch's eyebrows rose over her dark eyes.

"It's not what you're thinking," Azleah said quickly.

The witch smirked. "My thoughts are irrelevant. What is relevant is your father finding out."

"Don't call him that," Azleah said, spinning away from the witch and stalking to the window. "My true father is dead, and you've left a monster in his skin." She turned her head and studied the witch. "If you want to offer a gesture to gain my trust, this is the compromise. Only you and the Mad King can open the door, but you can open it for the guard to enter."

The witch stood looking down at the parchment, then looked back at Azleah and nodded. "Fine. Ten minutes."

"Tonight?"

The witch nodded. "Look for Hale Crue in an hour." Then she left.

Once again waiting till she was gone, Azleah rushed to the table and unrolled the parchment with impatience.

Dear Princess,

You asked me weeks ago if there was someone who'd captured my attention. I truthfully replied, no. Now, however, I find my concentration wanes during the day. I recall our conversations, the sounds, the words, pondering the nuance of what you've said and wondering if I might be making more meaning than I should. I imagine your smile. Then I chastise myself for it, because I'm but a palace guard and you are a princess. And perhaps I could earn your favor by freeing you, but I am unable to do even that. I imagine finding a way to rescue you. As I dream up possibilities, I find myself scolded by my superiors. So I renew my focus to not be removed from my detail, which would end my favorite time of the day and my ability to speak with you. You, dear princess, have captured my attention. I am filled with presumption—sharing this with you—but I find I cannot fulfill my duty with the unanswered question hanging over me. I know not your feelings, which I should think are not reciprocated, but if they are, you will make me the happiest of men.
Yours,
Crue

Azleah pressed the parchment to her heart and smiled. Then she spun in place, feeling the hope that had been born inside her weeks ago finally take flight. Too excited to eat, she moved restlessly about the confining room, putting things in order, brushing and re-plaiting her hair, then leaving it loose. Unsure where to wait, she paced, trying several different locations, testing what to do with her hands, her nerves fluttering in her stomach and heart.

In the end, she miscalculated the hour, because suddenly he was clearing his throat, and she was whirling in place to face him.

Crue stood in the doorway.

Her breath caught. "It's you." The words came out with the breath she'd momentarily lost.

He was beautiful. Tall, muscular in his uniform. Instead of brown hair, as she'd imagined, his was raven black, the tips of which brushed the top of his shoulders, though he'd tied the top back to keep it out of his eyes. And his eyes weren't green but intensely brown, so dark they appeared black, framed with thick brows. His jaw was square and clean-shaven, highlighting the beauty of the contours of his face. Her eyes dipped to his even mouth, his full lips curving up as he smiled.

"You are…" His words faded, then he dipped his head. "Your Highness."

"Not Your Highness, please. Not with you," she said. "Just Azleah."

He tipped his head slightly, his eyes lifting to her face.

Her heart raced in her chest. "Where's the witch?" she asked, trying to find something they could speak about to chase away the awkwardness between them.

He cleared his throat and straightened. "Waiting. We only have a few minutes." His eyes scanned her face, then her body before he met her gaze again. "Gods, you're beautiful." He clamped his mouth shut and shook his head. "Forgive my impertinence."

His words fluttered her heartbeat and, combined with the weeks upon weeks of speaking with him through the door, she could hardly speak. She wrung her hands together at her waist and blurted, "I got your message," holding up the parchment.

His cheeks darkened before his eyes fell, and he swiped a hand over his face. Then he moved, his leathers creaking, the ceremonial sword tapping against his thigh. "You think I'm a fool."

She took a step closer, shaking her head. "No."

He didn't lift his head, but his eyes met hers once more. Then he straightened and stepped toward her.

"I..." She paused, nervous and afraid, for she'd never felt the riot of sensations driving through her just then and wasn't sure how to interpret them, how to communicate them. If she even should. Only Crue had shared how he was feeling, so she sought that bravery. "I feel... so much. I feel... the same." Her cheeks heated at the admission, afraid that somehow, she'd been mistaken.

He took another step forward, his eyebrows arching high over his beautiful eyes. "You do?" His shocked grin filled her lungs.

She took another step toward him. "I can't sleep. Can't eat."

He moved closer. "Can't think. Can't concentrate."

"For thinking of you."

And suddenly he was there, standing in front of her, close enough to touch. His head tipped down to look at her, while hers tilted up.

"What are we to do?" she asked.

Crue reached out as if to touch her, but then stopped, awaiting her permission.

Azleah leaned toward his outstretched hand and closed her eyes when his calloused skin touched her cheek. It had been so long since anyone had chosen to touch her, and even longer since it had been someone she cared for, though this was the first time anyone had touched her for whom she felt attraction.

When she opened her eyes, she saw he was studying her. "This," he whispered.

Her heart expanded, making room for this person who'd been the first in so long to show her anything akin to affection, to love. She was starving for it.

Crue smiled, then pulled away, looking over his shoulder at a sound coming from the bottom of the stairs. When he turned back around, he retreated, but grabbed hold of her hand. "I have to go." With a squeeze, he backed toward the stairwell.

"I'll follow you," she said, "and then we can speak through the door."

He nodded and released her hand. "Wait. For the witch to leave." Then he disappeared around the stone curve. She listened to his steps growing fainter the further he descended the spiral stairs. That short time would never be enough with him.

By the time Azleah followed and pressed her palms to the door, feeling that familiar magic with its strange bite through her skin, she felt out of breath. It wasn't from her rush down the stairs but rather all the feelings she'd stored up for Crue.

"Are you there?"

"I am," he answered.

Azleah smiled and made herself comfortable on the floor as she had so many nights before, her body filled with more joy than she'd felt in as long as she could remember.

The next evening, and the next, and the next, the witch gave them time to be together. On the fifth, Crue asked to kiss her. Azleah allowed it, her heart beating like a drum inside her chest. When the witch gave them more time, they didn't waste it talking, since that could be done between the doors. Rather, there was more kissing, touching, and not enough connection.

The fourteenth evening after first meeting Crue face-to-face, the witch arrived and left dinner as usual—along with a small pouch.

"What is that?" Azleah asked, picking it up between two fingers.

The witch watched her. "Herbs. You need to drink it with your tea."

"Why?"

The witch leveled her dark gaze on Azleah. "To prevent pregnancy, Your Highness."

Shocked, Azleah sucked in a breath, though it would have been a lie to say she and Crue hadn't crossed several lines. "Oh."

"Should you require it." The witch turned to leave.

"How do you know?" It was strange to ask this of one of the parties responsible for her imprisonment, only Azleah didn't have anyone else to confide in.

The witch stopped and looked at Azleah over her shoulder.

Azleah took a step. "How do you know if you're ready for... that?" She had given it some thought—it was difficult not to think about the ways Crue made her feel when she was with him.

"Only you can answer that question," the witch replied and disappeared into the stairwell.

Azleah weighed the possibilities in her mind, unsure of herself but feeling in her heart of hearts that what she felt for Crue was real. Despite that feeling, by the time he appeared, she hesitated, though their last several meetings had been an instant meeting of hands and mouths.

"What is it?" he asked.

"What are we doing?"

Crue stepped closer and gathered her in his arms. She loved how safe she felt surrounded by his strength. "Being together—any way we can."

"I don't feel like this is me getting out of here." She stepped from his embrace.

"Why am I here?" he asked.

"Because I asked it of her."

"Why?"

"This allowance is a gesture of her goodwill on her part, so that I will trust her."

"Do you?"

Azleah's gaze slipped to the pouch and the tea she'd finished. When she looked at Crue, her heart expanded inside her chest. "I think I am beginning to."

He smiled. "That's a start."

She walked back to him and reached to unbuckle his sword belt.

Crue grasped her face between his calloused palms and kissed her as his sword fell to the floor, followed by another belt.

"Is this what we're doing?" he asked.

"Yes," she whispered into his mouth. "This is what I want. With you."

The appearance of the witch at midday was out of the ordinary. Azleah started from the book she was reading, jumping to her feet. "What are you doing here?"

The witch glanced over her shoulder; her dark eyes harried as she entered the room. The Mad King arrived on her heels.

"Oh," he breathed. The stairs had clearly exhausted him. A smile broke out on his unfamiliar face. "Alea."

"Azleah," she replied, shocked at the changes in him. Before, he had looked worn. Now he looked like a shade of himself. His skin was nearly transparent and loose as it hung from his bones. His hair was a shock of white, unkept and long like his beard, which had grown even longer. He frightened her.

He either didn't hear her or ignored her. "The witch has assured me you are well, but I wouldn't be deterred. I needed to see you for myself. It has been much too long."

Azleah's gaze jumped to the witch, who wasn't looking at her. She'd kept the Mad King away?

"I could forgo seeing you forever," Azleah replied.

His disconcerting eyes narrowed. "Witch?"

"My king?"

"My Alea doesn't speak to me so." His gaze shifted from Azleah to the witch. "What magic is this?"

"I have suggested you refrain from visiting, sire. The magic requires time," she explained, and though Azleah didn't know the witch well, she could see the annoyance in her countenance, in the taut way she said the words.

The Mad King's eyes flicked from the witch back to Azleah. "Is it working?"

"No," Azleah said.

"Yes," the witch said at the same time, narrowing her eyes at Azleah—a warning, it seemed, to play along. "Yes, Your Majesty. And it will take the remaining time to mature." The witch silenced Azleah's protest with a look. "But your visitation slows things–"

Azleah couldn't believe what she was hearing.

The witch was helping her. Just like she'd said.

"Then for what purpose is there to wait?" The king asked, stepping further into the tower room.

Azleah shrank back.

The witch shifted, moving to stand between Azleah and the king. "Sire. You want your true Alea, yes?"

A stranger's eyes—horrifying orbs of unnatural color—sought Azleah's, then cut back to the witch between them.

"Sire?" the witch prompted.

"Yes." He nodded. "Yes."

"Then you must allow the magic to work."

As one would with a small child, the witch turned him, grabbing hold of his arm and steering him back to the doorway and down the stairs. Azleah listened to them speak, though it was the hum of indecipherable sound rather than discernible conversation.

Her heart racing in her chest, she couldn't return to reading. Instead, she took the stairs and knocked on the door.

"Crue?"

"Who's there?" a stranger's voice asked.

Azleah fled up the stairs and crawled into her bed, filled with terror that exploded from her in sobs and tears. When a light touch landed on her back, she flinched and turned.

"Shhh." The witch sat on the side of the bed, her hands now in her lap. "I've calmed him and consulted the bones. It isn't time to go, but I think we need some added precautions to protect you. I'd like to give you some magic to wield."

Azleah sat up. "What kind of magic?"

"Prophecy Augur," she said. "To prevent something like today. You will see him coming before he comes to you. It will protect you from him."

"You can't do that already?"

She shook her head. "I can use my smooth tongue to soothe him—as you saw—but he's getting more erratic."

"And why don't we just do what we need to do to get me out, then?"

"Because the bones suggest that if we do it before the designated time, we fail."

"And I will not become like... him? By taking this magic?"

The witch shook her head.

"Fine. I will accept this gift."

"I will touch you," the witch said and lifted her hand, waiting.

When Azleah bent her head, the witch's hands—startingly soft—slid along the skin of her cheek, her fingers smoothing a lock of her hair from her face and tucking it behind Azleah's ear. Chills danced over her flesh—confusing—because she had felt it only once before with Crue. When Azleah raised her eyes to the witch, the woman's face hadn't changed but for her dark eyes, somehow darker.

The witch spoke words Azleah didn't recognize, and that chill on her head changed into a spike of brilliant heat settling deep into her body. Then it was gone as quickly as it had come.

"There," the witch said and drew back.

"How will I know if it worked?" Azleah asked.

"It will work. Concentrate on what you want to know, the magic should reveal those truths to you." The witch stood and retreated to the doorway.

"Will Crue come?"

The witch looked over her shoulder and nodded. "Same time."

Later, Azleah and Crue lay in her bed having just found comfort in one another's bodies. She was settled in the crook of his arm, her head tucked under his. His fingers drifted back and forth over her arm and shoulder blade as Azleah told him of her father's appearance.

"And on the day you had leave," she finished.

"I missed the excitement." Crue's fingers trailed her bare skin. "Were you frightened?"

"Yes, but..."

He adjusted so he could see her face. "What?"

"The witch helped me. I think, maybe, she's been trying to help me this whole time."

His eyebrows shifted over his eyes before he moved once

more, tucking her in closer against him, making a humming sound.

"And was your family well?" she asked.

"Yes. They asked me to return home."

Her heart constricted with both jealousy and sadness. She knew she couldn't ask him to remain for her sake, even if she longed for it. "And what did you tell them?"

"That I was beholden to my vow," he said, his voice lowered to a timbre that sent shivers down her spine as he maneuvered his thigh between hers. She made room for him as he settled in between her legs. "A very important vow," he added, placing a kiss on each cheeks.

"And what is that?"

"That I have vowed to protect the princess." He kissed her nose.

"What else does this vow entail?" she asked, smiling, for she could feel the length of him hardening.

He hummed and placed a kiss at the corner of her lips. "Lots of things."

"Like?"

Crue reached between them, taking himself in hand to slide through her slick heat. "Like pleasing her."

She sucked in a breath and tilted her hips to offer him more room.

He accepted the invitation, slowly sinking into her. "To make her feel... good."

"You do," she breathed, grabbing hold of his shoulder blades. "You do."

He kissed down her neck, moving slowly. "Azleah...This..."

Suddenly, a bright heat sliced through her vision. She sucked in a breath as an image of the Mad King darted through her mind. He was stalking through the corridor. She started, drawing away from Crue.

"What is it? Azleah?" The concern in Crue's voice pulled her back.

"The king. He's coming."

Crue pulled out of her body and jumped from the bed.

"The witch is at the door?" she asked, looking about to where she might hide him, but her room had no such place.

Crue stumbled across the room, a foot in a pant leg, stammering about needing to get to the door. "Where is he?" He buttoned his pants and shoved his head into his tunic.

"Somewhere in the corridor."

He slid the breastplate on, and Azleah helped him buckle it as he fastened his many weapons. Then he was running out the door, and Azleah stood, naked, watching him go. But he came back to press a needy kiss to her lips, before disappearing down the stairs one more.

Azleah waited, her heart slamming against her chest, her breath shallow and fearful, but seconds, then minutes, then an hour passed and nothing happened.

The king never appeared.

Crue didn't return, either, so she was left to worry until the witch appeared, announcing she'd appeased the king.

Crue did return the next night, and the night after that. And so it went for weeks, Azleah losing herself in Crue, giving herself to him and taking what he offered, falling deeper and deeper into love.

Then one day, when the witch brought her dinner, rather than offer Azleah a story about the kingdom, she said, "The bones have decided I must offer you another gift. Prophecy has saved you—and Hale Crue—from discovery, but I wonder if you might be able to use a different gift to sway the king."

"Like your words?"

"Somewhat," the witch said. "Perhaps the power to influence his thoughts?"

Liking the sound of that, Azleah nodded. "How?"

The witch stepped up on the dais in front of Azleah and said, "Dream walking. The power to infiltrate his dreams and speak with him. Influence him."

This sounded like something manageable. "This won't make me like him?"

The witch shook her head. "But it is... darker magic."

"As long as I won't lose myself, I will accept it."

"Lie down on the bed," the witch said.

So Azleah did, her heart's rhythm turning tinny in her chest with anticipation. The witch touched her once more, this time in the center of throat, then running a finger down her body in a straight line as she spoke her strange words. The same heat infiltrated Azleah's body as before, slithering through her until it settled around her spine. The witch's finger stopped at Azleah's heart, just between her breasts.

When the witch was done, she stepped away. "Have you been taking the herb?"

"Yes. Every night with dinner."

The witch nodded. "Good." She stood, turned, then left the room without another word.

Azleah fell into a routine, with the maid, the witch, and now with Crue, her gift of prophecy keeping them from discovery. One night, after Crue had returned to his post, Azleah—so very tired—closed her eyes, only to drift into a dream that took her deep within the confines of the castle to a place she had never seen, where she found the Mad King sleeping restlessly atop a bed.

The sensation of being drawn into something grabbed hold of her, and when she looked around, she stood in a garden, with her father—not yet the Mad King, but the father she remembered holding her hand. He was staring at her, a sly smile upon his lips. "Are you sure, Alea?" he asked. "This could change everything."

"I'm not Alea," Azleah said inside the dream. "I'm Azleah."

Her father's smile faded, and the brilliant garden withered and wilted around them, turning black. He shook his head. "Alea. Why would you say such a thing?"

"Because it is the truth. Have you not told me to always tell you true?" Azleah asked.

"But–" The king looked around then, at the garden landscape ugly and decrepit. His face began to age. "That can't be." He glanced at his hands. Startled, he yelled as they withered before his eyes like the garden.

"Know me, Father," she said.

And suddenly she was torn from the dream, racing across the seam of reality before starting awake in her own bed. She sat up, clutching her chest, her body coated in sheen of sweat as nausea overtook her. Bolting for the pot, she eliminated everything, then crawled back into bed, unable to move as morning overtook the room. The maid came and went.

Minutes or hours later, she had no notion, there was a strange noise at the doorway.

Azleah raised her head from her pillow.

The Mad King stood there watching, then he shuffled across the room.

"Where is the witch?" Azleah asked, unable to move, her body weak.

The king said nothing, the deep lines in his face somehow deeper with his frown. He stopped at her bedside and looked down at her.

Azleah raised the covers to her chin. "I'm not my mother. Know me, Father."

He sighed, a great heaving of... Azleah couldn't name it... then turned and left the room in great haste, leaving Azleah's heart racing and hope blooming in her chest.

When the witch came later with dinner, Azleah was bursting with it. "Then he left," she finished. "I think... I think the dreaming worked."

"Perhaps for a moment," the witch said, pushing a dish toward her. "His purpose was unchanged when I saw him today."

Azleah picked up the bowl of steamed carrots and ate. "Is there magic that might be more lasting?"

The witch settled her hands in her lap. "Magic is a fickle servant," she said. "You might think it is the answer, but are we not in this predicament because of magic?"

"Yes," Azleah said slowly and took another bite. "But you said to yourself we will need magic to get out of it. We're just waiting for the right time."

The witch sat forward. "I did."

"What did the bones say?" Azleah asked, setting down

the dish and standing. Unable to stay still, she paced, awaiting the witch's wisdom.

"That you would seek another gift, and I can give it, but I find myself... wary."

Azleah stopped. "Why?"

"I have been careless with your father. I don't wish to harm you. Come. Eat."

For the first time, Azleah looked upon the witch not as the object of her torment but as a trusted friend. She sat once more and picked up her fork. "I appreciate that, and this is my choice. I need to protect myself."

The witch measured Azleah with her gaze before her shoulders fell, as if resigned to the inevitable. "As you wish," she said. "But after you eat."

So Azleah ate, and when she was done, the witch stood. "A warning, princess, this magic—a third gift—can be heavy to carry."

"What will it be this time?" Azleah asked, excited.

"Wisdom Oracle," she said. "To rule words and to harness knowing."

Azleah stood. "That might make it last?"

"It is the gift that I have used on your father. I am gifting it to you. I will lose it as you gain it, just as I have all the others."

"Wait." Azleah tilted her head to study the witch. "You've been giving me your own magical gifts."

The witch nodded. "It is the least I can do for the pain I have caused." She extended a hand. "Come."

Azleah took the witch's hand, letting the witch turn her so they both faced the same direction. Then the witch stepped in closer, fitting her body into the spaces made by Azleah's back and curves. Azleah's breath caught in her lungs at the nearness of the witch, at the way those warm chills of her touch danced across her skin.

"What..."

"Hush," the witch said, her breath near Azleah's ear. The woman slid her hands around Azleah's waist and pressed her palms against Azleah's belly. As she said her words, the bright, hot warmth built inside Azleah, flowing through the witch's touch. The witch's hands shifted a touch lower, spanning the space just above Azleah's pelvis, and the heat radiated, until the witch made a sound.

Suddenly, her touch was gone, leaving Azleah so cold she shivered.

"How will I know if it worked?" Azleah asked, and turned, but the witch was gone.

Later, Crue visited, nearly out of breath when he burst through her doorway. Azleah waited for him, wrapped only in a blanket.

He stopped abruptly. "Oh. Gods, you're beautiful. I missed you," he breathed and started with his buckles.

A vision danced across her mind of Crue removing the

witch's clothes. She blinked and watched him take off his breastplate.

"Is the witch waiting?" Azleah asked.

Crue's eyes flitted up, then quickly away. There was a breath of hesitation, then he smiled. "Yes." The thud of his breastplate on the floor cut the word short.

He was lying. She wasn't sure how she knew and wondered if perhaps it was the new magic inside her. "What aren't you telling me?"

Crue stopped, his pants unfastened, his shirt untucked. "What?"

Azleah walked toward him, the blanket dragging behind her as she did. "You just lied."

"I didn't. The witch is watching."

Azleah shook her head. "I asked if she was waiting."

Crue took a deep breath. "What's this?"

"What aren't you telling me?"

Crue straightened, his arms at his sides. He curled his hands into fists, then hung his head. "I knew giving you these gifts would change things."

And then his form changed.

His black hair grew, his body leaned and lengthened, and his face morphed until the witch stood before Azleah, dark, knowing eyes and all.

"Oh," Azleah gasped. She fell backward onto the bed. "You?"

"Am I?" the witch asked, and the change began again. Her face transformed into Crue again, then aged, his dark hair sleeker and threaded with bits of silver. The masculine body filled back in until a man stood before her, a different Crue, but older with the same dark eyes filled with knowing like the witch.

"Who are you?" Azleah whispered.

"One and the same."

"Crue?"

"And the witch. This" –the man waved a hand in front of him– "is my true form."

"But–" Azleah stammered. "I don't understand."

The man, no longer clothed in Crue's uniform but head to toe in black, walked across the room and pulled a chair away from the table. He waved a hand at the dinner tray, and it was refilled with fresh fruit, cheese, and bread. "Come. Sit." He lifted a goblet of wine to his lips.

Azleah did, frightened but curious, her breath coming in shallow pants.

The man set a goblet in front of her. "It will be fine for the baby."

"Baby?"

"It would seem the herbs weren't as effective as we'd hoped." His eyes dropped to her belly.

"What?" Azleah pressed her palms to her stomach, her gaze following her hands.

"I'd like to tell you a story." The man smiled—Crue's smile—and pushed the tray closer to her.

"A story?" she asked, slowly. She suddenly couldn't find her bearings and felt as though she might be floating outside her body.

"I came to your father because he summoned me after the death of your mother. My magic is unparalleled," the man said, "and I relish the opportunity to demonstrate my prowess. As I traveled, I was regaled with stories of your parents' great love. My magic, of course, cannot summon this, and while I am content in most things, I should like a great love story. I found myself jealous but curious about this great love, so I agreed."

Azleah watched him pop a grape into his mouth.

"When I arrived and found your father's bereaved state, I decided it was only fair to support his desire to speak once more with your mother. Who am I to stand in the way to true love, after all? We dabbled in the darkest of magics to find a tether, and I eventually found a way for them to speak across time and space. But when your father returned, he wasn't the same. His grief had taken on a manic shine, no longer content to just speak with her. He asked for her resurrection."

"And you said 'yes.'"

"I said no," the man said. "This is a kind of magic that can't be done. And I was set to leave, only I saw... you." His eyes connected to Azleah, and the depth of feeling in them raced down her spine.

"Me?"

He nodded. "At the sight of you, I felt strange. It was as if the world had suddenly begun spinning properly but sent me careening in the opposite direction. A feeling with which I was wholly unfamiliar, and I wondered if this was what was meant by being lovestruck. So I lied to your father and told him that I might know of a witch who could help him."

"You are the witch."

He nodded. "I stayed, to remain close to you. To see and learn about love."

"And you drove him mad."

"No. No." The man shook his head. "What has become of your father is a result of his own choices. I offered him magic, told him the consequences–"

"Like you've done with me?"

"Yes. Only..."

Azleah stood and turned away from him, moving to the window. "You tricked me. You pretended this whole time."

"Would you have listened had I revealed myself from the beginning?"

Azleah didn't look at him. She knew she wouldn't have, but she didn't say it. She felt... angry. Hurt. Foolish. She had fallen in love with Crue. Had given her heart, her body, her soul to a figment. Tears filled her eyes, but she wouldn't let them fall.

She folded her hands over her belly. A baby.

"And what is it you want of me?" She turned back to him. "Because that is what this is all about, yes? You want my kingdom? My riches?"

He offered her a patient but short grin. "Oh, Azleah, use the wisdom I have given you. I can acquire these things without you." He stood and crossed the room to stand before her. "Search your body... your heart, your mind, your instinct, and know me."

"I loved Crue. Not you."

"I am Crue." He reached out and pressed his palm to her heart.

It fluttered with feeling, and the rest of her came alive just as she had with each touch of the witch—with Crue—with each of his touches. Her feelings for Crue overshadowed her bitterness, and her mind opened.

"I want you," he said, then slid his hand to cover her belly. "I want our child."

She staggered away from him. "I don't know you."

"You do." He sighed. "Search your heart and consider all I've told you. The bones say it is time to go. I would like to free you from your tower. I promised this... as Crue. This I will do, either way, but I hope you will choose me." He paused as if allowing that to sink in. Then he said, "I'll return tomorrow and seek your answer."

She watched the man disappear down the stairs. Then, and only then, did she finally let herself cry.

The next morning, instead of the maid, the man—older Crue, as she'd begun thinking of him—appeared in her doorway, only he was more frantic than she'd ever witnessed the witch or her Crue. Dressed all in black like the night before, he hurried to Azleah's bedside and fell to his knees. Her Crue was in his face, and her heart pinched, leaning toward him, but she was still hurt and angry by his duplicity.

"Your answer?"

"You'll get me out of here?"

"You'll get yourself out of here. I will give you the magic to do it, and I would like to care for you and our baby. I mean… if you'll let me." His head fell forward, his dark hair obscuring his eyes.

Azalea had spent the night crying and knew she was out of options.

"What do I call you?"

"Crue."

She sat up and swung her legs over the side of the bed next to where he knelt. As much as she wanted to be stubborn, there wasn't room for it. She needed to get out of this tower room, and she needed to be away from her father. And this magician—this Crue—was willing to help her. "You are promising to help me leave my father?" It was the thing she most wanted to hear.

He looked up at her, hope softening the severity of his face.

He was her Crue once more.

"Yes."

"Then I will go with you."

He breathed a sigh of relief. "We're out of time."

And so they made a plan.

"The king is coming for you tonight," Crue said, "and I won't be able to intervene, because I will need to restructure the spell. Which is why I need to give you one more gift."

"What is it?"

"Time Runner."

"And what will that do?"

"You'll be able to skip through time, but it is very important that you keep in mind where you need to be and when. Time running is dangerous." Crue put his hands on her once more and said words she didn't know. The heat of the magic seeped through her, joining with her body.

"And where should I think to go?" Azleah asked.

"I have a cabin in the Eppers."

"The Haunted Bog?"

"You've been there?"

"Yes."

"There. That's where you'll go. And it isn't haunted." Grabbing a piece of their old parchment, he conjured a writing implement, then sketched a map, wrote out directions, and pointed to a spot. "This is where you need to go. I will meet you there."

"I have to go by myself?"

He took her face between his palms. "I have every faith you can do this. But you must wait for your father. It will give me time to work on the spell."

She could have said no, but that version still left her trapped. This seemed the best means to get what she needed.

Out.

She could only think about that, especially now with a child. Her trust, her worries didn't matter, so she nodded.

He pressed a soft kiss to her cheek.

Her Crue—at least, that was what she told herself.

Beyond escaping from the tower, the palace, her father, she would take things with him one moment at a time. Crue would have to regain her trust, and this would go a long way. He had always promised to help her escape, and now he was, even if his methods left something to be desired.

"I'll see you at the cabin." Then he turned and left Azleah to wait.

Her father arrived just as the sun kissed the horizon. "Alea."

Azleah turned to face him. "I am not Alea."

Anger marred his features as red flushed his face. "Enough of this!" He started across the tower room. "I shall not wait any longer. The witch is a liar!"

Azleah had run out of time. She shut her eyes, thought of the Eppers, of the spot that Crue had pointed out. "Right now," she whispered. "Right now."

With the sound of a shutting door, a whirl of air swept up and blocked her father's yell. When she opened her eyes, she stood next to the river that fed the Epper Marsh.

The Marsh, which looked more like a waterless mish mash of tufts of green grass and muddy bog, stretched on and on. The river didn't run through the marsh but veered off, bordering it as it flowed to the farmlands of Echo. On the horizon, she could see the shadow of the Narrow Mountains.

Azleah turned in a circle and shivered at the chill in the

air. Her mouth opened with noiseless awe, then she whispered, "It worked." She squeaked with joy and added a little dance, then remembered the map, which she dug from her pocket. The sun was falling quickly, and she needed the light. She followed Crue's directions, turning toward the cluster of trees that eventually turned into the woods. It was there she'd find the house.

"Look for the craggy lone tree" he'd said. *"You'll turn toward the hills there."*

So she did, following his directions until a quaint house materialized in the woods. Though it was small, it looked as if it belonged nestled between giant trees, a part of them, the wood slick with a mossy sheen, its roof hidden in the bowers of the branches. Lamps were lit in the two windows, and smoke drifted from the chimney.

She followed the stone path to the door painted a vibrant shade of red and knocked.

It cracked open to a wrinkled eye, then swung wide, revealing an old woman. Her silver hair was threaded with black, her shoulders hunched, a cane in her hand. "Who are you?" she demanded, her voice coarse.

Azleah's heart thudded in her chest, wondering if she'd come to the wrong house, but there didn't seem to be another. "Azleah. Crue told me to meet him here."

"Who the hell is Crue?"

Azleah's mouth opened, then shut. "Um." She

swallowed and looked back over her shoulder at the darkened woods, knowing she didn't have anywhere else to go. "He... works at the castle. In Echo Landing."

The woman laughed. "Work? Is this a joke?"

"No." Azleah bristled.

The woman's eyes narrowed, and she shuffled a few steps to look out the door, glanced around, then shuffled back inside. "Come on then." She waited for Azleah to enter, then shut the door. "Crue, huh? Is that the name he's using now? He get you pregnant?"

Azleah's cheeks reddened, but she didn't answer. "He said to meet him here. That he would help..."

The old woman clicked her tongue. "That's what he tells them all. He has no intention of helping you raise your... issue."

"But–"

"He said he loves you?"

It wasn't until the old woman asked that Azleah had ever thought about it, but upon mention, she realized neither of them had ever said those words, even if she'd felt them. Though she wasn't sure she still felt them, considering his trick.

"He won't," the old woman said with authority. "He can't. He's sold his soul and gave up his heart."

"What?"

At a sound beyond the doorway, Azleah jumped.

"Hide," the old woman hissed, pushing Azleah into a small alcove of the hearth behind the potbelly woodstove. "Hush and listen. You will see," she said, then disappeared from Azleah's sight.

Though Azleah couldn't see, she heard the door open and steps start over the wooden floor, stilling suddenly.

"Aunt Mercy." It was Crue's voice—older Crue, of course—filled with a sound Azleah couldn't identify. She suppressed the urge to jump from her hiding place and rush into his arms, and instead forced herself to listen, just as the old woman had suggested. It was a knowing of some kind, a hesitation, and the hint of a voice inside her telling her to wait.

"As you see," Mercy said. "No thanks to you."

He scoffed. "I thought–"

"What? That I wasn't coming back?"

"You left for the sea." Crue's steps sounded on the floor once more. "I set you up nicely there. You didn't like the cottage?"

"It was a dump. So I have returned. Besides, it was too cold and too wet."

"Joyous occasion, then," he answered, but his voice didn't sound joyful. "I'm expecting... someone."

"A girl."

"Is she here?"

"No. She came and left. I saved you from having to

break the news. Or should I say, I saved her."

"What news is that?" Crue asked. A creaking sounded, hinting that he might have taken a seat.

"That you won't raise the bastard." The old woman's cane hit the floor as she said each word. "How many more will you hunt?"

Hunt?

The air changed as if all the oxygen was being deprived from the room, compressing Azleah's lungs. The light dimmed, slipping toward a gray twilight as if the sun shone through a thick cloudbank.

The old woman coughed.

"You," Crue's voice took on a horrifying edge, "have meddled for the last time, Aunt."

"I am your kin!" She wheezed. "I raised you."

"The sea cottage was a kindness, and you have trounced on my goodwill for the last time."

More coughing. "I cannot see you kill another. I cannot," she choked.

Azleah covered her mouth with her hand and squeezed her eyes shut. *Kill?*

"I have saved her from a horrible existence as her father's bride!" Crue yelled.

"Only to die by yours?" the old woman squeaked.

There was movement, a slide, a lurch, a step. The old woman coughed, then there was a thud, as if something had fallen. A gasp for breath.

Azleah held hers.

"Where is she?" Crue demanded.

"Or will you finally come to? Raise your child. I can't," Mercy's voice broke.

"Can't what?" Crue's voice was nearly unrecognizable. Azleah knew it had to be him only because she knew he was the only other person in the cabin. "I will do what I always do. I have given her gifts she must return, and she is godblood. I will be a god."

"You will consume them? Like the others?"

"Where did she go?"

"You are an abomination," the old woman spat.

"A very powerful one." He paused. "Where is she?" he shouted.

Tears sprang to Azleah's eyes, and she squeezed them shut. With her hands pressed to her belly, she thought of her mother, of her mother's burial mound, of Remembrance Valley.

"Mother," she whispered, and just as had happened earlier, a door shut on the sound of Crue—the wizard—and the old woman yelling and struggling. Azleah opened her eyes and crouched in the darkness before the shadowy swell of an earthen mound. Then she buried her face in her hands and cried.

"I have nowhere to go," she sobbed, and after her tears

had subsided, she wiped her eyes. She glanced at the shadow of the castle, at the tower where she'd been held captive. "But I am out," she whispered and ran her hand over her still flat belly. "And I have magic. I will do everything in my power to protect you," she vowed.

"Azleah?"

Her head whirled at the voice. It was too dark to see anything, but she knew it was him.

"Azleah? Are you here? This is where you always went... before."

She held her breath.

"My aunt Mercy said she sent you away. She's..." He paused.

She could make out his footsteps in the loam.

"Look, she probably said some things that sounded crazy. The old woman is senile. I took her to the coast, where I thought the sea air would help her, but... Azleah?"

She squeezed her eyes shut and lay down, her back against her mother's burial mound. "Not here," she whispered and imagined leaving, imagined anywhere else. It started with the color green and sunshine before fear grabbed hold.

The door shut once more.

When she opened her eyes this time, she was sitting in a dense, green wood unlike anything she'd ever seen before. She stood and turned in a circle, looking up at the sun shining through the green leaves.

"Hello!" a kind voice called.

Azleah whirled, afraid that Crue had followed her somehow, but it wasn't his voice, and the forest around her was empty.

"Down here," the voice said.

Azleah looked down at her feet and there—no bigger than her thumb—was a man. Startled, she fell backward.

"Oh! I didn't mean to startle you, woman! Apologies," he said, and climbed up onto her ankle using the holes in her boot and laces to help himself. Then he traversed the length of her dress to her knee, where he stopped.

"You're... what are you?" she stammered. "A sprite?"

"Not a sprite," he said. "Just a man." He grinned, and his eyes—as green as the spring leaves around them—twinkled. Brown hair stuck out from beneath his tiny blue hat, with a brown beard to match.

"But you're so..."

"Small?"

She nodded.

"I might say the same of you, though the opposite. You are rather large, yes?" He sat, settling into a groove made by the fabric of her skirt. "It's a matter of perspective."

"I suppose you're right. Is everyone in this land like you?"

"You're not from around here, then?"

She shook her head.

"Unfortunately not. I am rather small." He laughed.

She couldn't help but giggle even as tears stung her eyes. "But why?"

"Why am I small? My parents wished this on me. They had me when they were older, you see, and they never expected to have a child, so when I was born, they wished for me to remain small. Instead of growing bigger, I began to grow smaller as I aged, and here I am."

"Magic."

"Which is probably why you can hear me at all. Someday, I will grow so small I will cease to be at all." Despite the implication of the words, he offered that easy smile once more and held out a tiny hand. "I'm Tomas."

Azleah held out a finger. Despite everything careening through her, his touch brought joy. "It's nice to meet you, Tomas. I'm..." She paused, knowing she had to leave her past behind. Glancing around, her gaze settled on a bush filled with bright red berries, and she thought of the red door of the cabin. "I'm Scarlett, and I'm afraid I'm lost."

"Well, good thing you nearly fell on me." He stood on her knee once more, dusting himself off. "Despite my size, I am a big help. Put me on your shoulder, and let's be off. We have some lunch to look after. Then maybe I can help you find which way to go."

Scarlett

"Are you well?" Tomas asked her from his perch on her shoulder hidden in her hair.

They had been traveling together for months, and Tomas, despite his diminutive size, used his wiles to find them what they needed. They always had a place to sleep and food for their bellies. They'd slept in barns, inns, and offered bedrooms. They'd been given coins and livestock to trade. They'd had traveling companions who'd offered places: caravans, performers, farmers off to market. Scarlett had wanted for nothing.

Tomas's craftiness made it easy to trick people into offering necessities to keep them alive. It wasn't a life she'd grown up living, but she was free, and she'd never felt more cared for. Though they were always moving, and the wear and tear was beginning to tax her growing frame, she had made a friend in Tomas. They laughed together, told stories, shared insecurities and vulnerabilities. Somewhere along the path between meeting Tomas and the six months since, her heart had shifted from friendship toward something deeper. Six months of running from Crue. Six months with Tomas as her guide. Six months to grow to love him more than she'd ever loved anyone.

"Scarlett?" he asked once more.

With her heart thumping a powerful awareness, the baby inside her moved as if in agreement with her choice. She smiled, placing her hand on her belly.

"The baby?" Tomas asked, concerned.

"She's okay."

"She?"

"Yes. The witch from the woods told me. From my dreams. Remember?"

He hummed a sound. "Right. The witch." She could hear his skepticism, and that made her smile even more. He was a man no bigger than her thumb.

She continued walking. "It isn't as if I have much of a choice when a sorcerer is after me. After the baby." She grabbed hold of her protruding stomach protectively. She'd calculated she had a couple more months to go. "We need to find a place where we can stop. Settle," she said. "This baby will be here before we know it. We have to prepare."

"We?" Tomas asked, a smile in his tone.

She blushed. "I–"

"Stop," he said. "Of course I'll be there. There is nowhere I would rather be."

Suddenly a vision sliced through her mind, and she stumbled, grabbing hold of a tree trunk to keep her upright. She hissed in pain.

"What is it? Scar?" Tomas asked, but his voice receded as a thick impenetrable darkness spread around them, exactly where they stood on a trail in the heart of a wood somewhere she didn't know. She had used her gifts so frequently she'd lost track. Prophecy, time running, dreaming. They'd become second nature even if she didn't know how to control them. It was as if the magic itself was trying to keep her safe from Crue.

Heart pounding, she labored to straighten, turning toward the forest, her back against the tree.

"What is it?" Tomas repeated.

"He's here. He found us."

"Milady?" one of the two men traveling with them asked. Tomas had used his smallness to convince the farmers Scarlett was a good-luck fairy by pretending to make one of their oxen talk. She glanced at him and at the other young man, his son, suddenly worried for them.

As if she had summoned him, Crue stepped from the shadows. Young Crue. He looked as she remembered him, dressed in the soldier's regalia of her kingdom. Every choice the sorcerer made was a manipulation of her emotions.

One of the farmers made a sound of surprise, pulling his hat from his head. "Sir," he said. "We have papers."

Crue ignored the farmer. "My love. I've found you. Are you happy to see me?"

The second of the two farmers, holding onto the harness of the oxen looked between Scarlett and Crue. "Is this your babe's father?"

"Yes." Crue's eyes measured her form greedily, looking at her pregnant belly. "You look well."

"This is him?" Tomas asked, his voice determined in her ear.

She nodded.

Frowning, Crue tilted his head. "Whose voice is that?" His eyes jumped to the two farmers, then back to Scarlett. "Who is speaking?"

"Me!" Tomas boomed, surprising Scarlett, his voice so imposing it startled the birds in the trees around them that they took flight.

The farmers fell to their knees. "The ox is speaking!"

Crue looked from the oxen to Scarlett. "That is no ox." He crossed the woods toward her and the men. "And who are you?" He bent, turned, adjusted as he looked for Tomas.

"A touch of magic, it would seem."

"One who sees what's true."

"And what truth do you see?" Crue asked, lifting the tarpaulin tied over the farmers' wagon.

"One who is noble, and one who isn't."

"I think we know which one I am." Crue chuckled, then twirled in place, arms outstretched, and laughed louder. He reached out and touched the man closest to him—the older of the two—and Scarlett watched the farmer crumple to the ground. Dead.

The second man yelped, dropped to his knees, and bowed his head, his mouth moving silently in prayer. "Father," he cried, grabbing hold of the older man and dragging him into his lap.

Scarlett's eyes rose to Crue's. "You are cruel."

"A death-touch spell." He wiped his hands together and grinned before turning his head to gaze at Scarlett once more. "Rather simple, actually. Perhaps, faceless voice, you should show yourself."

"No," Scarlett said, her mind drifting toward the witch she'd been dreaming of the last several weeks, the witch she'd told Tomas about. She knew they couldn't use magic against Crue, he was much too adept and powerful. Her only choice was as it had been for the last six months, run as far as she could and hide, but this time there would be help waiting.

"I insist." Crue took a step toward her, his hand out. "Or you and the babe will face the same fate, my love."

"No. We won't," she replied, lifting her chin, calling Crue's bluff. "You need us." She covered her belly with her hand and glanced at the young farmer cowering in anguish over his dead father.

Tomas stepped out from under her hair. "Here I am."

"No!" Scarlett said at the same time.

Surprised, Crue took a step back, a grin bursting on his face along with a surprised laugh of delight, as if Tomas were a prank being played upon him. "What is this magic?"

"A gift," Tomas replied.

"For me?" Crue asked.

"For her."

Crue's amusement grew dark, his eyes flying from Tomas's face to Scarlett's. "After all we've shared together, this is why you stay away. I loved you."

"You have no love for me."

Crue's brows collapsed together, then softened. "You carry our child. And yes, I was angry you ran," he confessed, moving slowly toward her. His lips puffed together in a pout, but then he grinned and clapped his hands together. "But let us not focus on the past, and instead the present and future. I'm overjoyed that I have found you. That I get to be a father. We can be a happy family."

Scarlett hummed a noise and took a step back. "Except

for the fact you would consume us upon the babe's birth. You want my godblood and the babe's."

Crue stilled, his brows furrowing over his dark eyes. Then they smoothed out. "Your gifts?" He scoffed. "Gifts I've given you."

She didn't move, wary and unsure how the wizard might react. But she knew what to do now, had practiced with the dream witch how to use the time run to take her, the baby, and Tomas where they could insulate themselves from the wizard's sight. She just had to do it before he acted, had to wait for the right moment.

"And what do your gifts tell you now?" he asked, taking another step toward her.

"That you are darkness, consuming everything in your path."

"And you and our baby are a part of that power," he replied.

"I'll create a diversion," Tomas whispered. "Then you run."

"No, Tom," Scarlett said. "I can do this."

"Tom?" Crue's head snapped around, looking at Tomas. He laughed. "A small name for a small man."

"And yet, so much more of a man than you," Scarlett replied, and just as she'd done over and over, she closed her eyes and slid through the seam of the realm in between worlds, a door snapping shut behind her, cutting off Crue's enraged bellow as she and Tomas disappeared.

But this time she didn't stop, hopscotching through various realms toward the woods where she would find Baba, the witch in the woods, losing Crue in a trail of time. She envisioned the gnarled tree with the woman's face from her dream and whispered, "There."

When she stopped, Tomas still clinging to her, she collapsed into the loam at the foot of the gnarled tree.

"Tomas," she cried when she felt him fall from her shoulder.

"I'm here," he reassured her.

Then, just in case Crue's powers had let him follow, she crawled into a thicket of brush to hide, and there she cried with Tomas to comfort her.

It wasn't until her belly grumbled with the need to eat that she and Tomas emerged from their hiding place. The forest had been silent, but the tree with the woman's face stood sentinel, a great hulking beast of a tree, gnarled with an unnatural grace.

Scarlett struggled to her feet and called out, "Baba. I'm here. I have come."

The face in the tree moved, shifting as if made of clay, the wood groaning under the strain.

Startled, Scarlett gasped.

"Scarlett," Tomas warned, pulling at her skirt with all his might.

The wood of the tree crackled and fractured open, spewing bright light. From the light, an old woman materialized, old in a way that made Scarlett think of the beginning of time, and the tree stood whole behind the witch once more. She was hunched in her clothes, rags hanging from her body as if they were layers of her rather than a fabric covering. Her hair was a bright silver, nearly white, obscuring her face. Though Scarlett couldn't make out her features, she had the impression Baba's eyes were glowing orbs of darkness.

"Scarlett. It's still Scarlett, is it not?"

"Yes, Baba."

"Your baby has reached the nearing," the old witch said. "Just in time."

Scarlett spread a palm over her belly. "Yes. It's time to hide," she'd said. "I have to keep her safe."

Tomas scurried up a tree to a branch where he could see Scarlett's face. "Why are you doing this? With her? Nothing is free."

Of course Scarlett knew this, but she'd had to take measure of the lesser of two evils.

"I need to keep her safe," she replied. "Please, Tomas. I have trusted you, and you have kept us safe. Now I need you to trust me."

"And what is it you require?" Tomas asked the witch.

The old woman looked at him, tilted her head, and

waited as if her body remained but her mind traveled. Then she said, "I have seen. And in the end, I will be rewarded."

"I don't–" Tomas started, his tiny hand pointing at the witch.

"Trust me?" She cackled, her head tipping back as she did. "That is a good thing, small man," the witch told Tomas. "It will be necessary for her and the babies."

"Babies?" both Scarlett and Tomas asked.

"But" –the witch tapped her chin– "you cannot stay this small. Time to reverse the wish." She wiggled her fingers.

"Wait!" Scarlett cried.

The witch looked at her, her hands frozen in front of her, violet threads of light intertwined between her fingers.

"But I love him just this way," Scarlett admitted quietly.

Tomas straightened on his tree branch. "Love me?"

Scarlett lifted her head to meet his gaze, her cheeks hot. "I'd wished to tell you," she said, embarrassed, "but not by blurting it out so."

The witch interrupted. "He must. If you are to hide, he must be able to blend in at your side."

"Yes," Tomas agreed, nodding, his eyes never wavering from Scarlett's. "I should like that."

Scarlett's heart picked up its wayward beat as her cheeks grew hotter.

With a muttered spell, the violet lightning burst from

the witch's hands and Tomas began to grow, and grow, and grow, his clothes tearing from his body, leaving him naked and exposed. The branch on which he was perched broke, and he fell to the ground, into the brush. He grew and grew, his body expanding.

He yelled out with pain.

Scarlett cried, "Tomas!" and surged forward, but the witch stopped her with a hand, her power creating an invisible wall between them.

"Let it happen," Baba said.

And still he grew.

Eventually Baba's lightning ceased, and the forest was quiet—no birds, no breeze, nothing.

"Tomas?" Scarlett whimpered, suddenly afraid she'd made a terrible mistake.

"I'm here," he groaned, reassuring her as he always did. He moved in the brush, getting to his feet.

Scarlett tilted her head up to look at him—at least a foot taller than her—the size of a tree, it seemed. She swallowed. She'd thought him handsome for so long, only now it was difficult to take in the beauty of his face in such visible relief. Her body heated as she looked at him, and then she realized she was staring too long and removed her cloak, handing it to him.

Baba laughed, her cackle an unnerving sound. "Babies."

But Scarlett barely noticed it, unable to look away from Tomas, her heart a rapid beat in her throat. Despite the heavy burden of the baby inside her body, her heart beat for the man standing before her.

He took her offered cloak, his skin pinkening with a blush as he wrapped the fabric around his hips. Then he stepped forward, grabbed hold of Scarlett, and pulled her into his embrace, pressing his face into the space between her neck and shoulder. "This," he whispered. "I've wanted to do this."

Scarlett melted into the rightness of his embrace, her hands grasping hold of the strong muscles of his back.

"There's more work to do," Baba said. "There's a village at the edge of the woods called Sevens." She pulled a small, glass bottle from inside her cloak, still talking. "You'll go there so that you aren't far from me." Her eyes had jumped between them, and she'd grinned once more. "Yes, you will need me, it seems." She nodded, her gaze clouding. "Yes. You will need me."

Then she shook herself back to the moment and held out the bottle.

Scarlett took the small vial, not much bigger than her palm. "And then?"

"Build a life," the witch said. "It is what you have wanted, yes?"

"Yes, Baba." Scarlett looked at Tomas and when he

smiled, she grinned but struggled to keep connected, suddenly nervous.

"That potion is for the wards." Baba rustled through a rucksack that had suddenly materialized against her hip.

"Wards?" Tomas asked.

"A protective spell to hide your home, the power she carries, the babies." The witch stopped, pulling out a red ribbon woven with a second ribbon shimmering pink, with violet and golden threads as she leveled a stern look at Scarlett. "But beware, if you tell the truth, the ward will fail."

Scarlett nodded.

"This is for the baby," the witch continued, holding out the ribbon. "It will hide her from the wizard's sight."

Scarlett spread the silky trinket across her palm.

"The same applies to this," the witch said. "Should you ever reveal the truth fueling the spells, they will fail and expose everything."

"To remain hidden, I must conceal it?"

"Yes. There is one other thing that will break the ribbon's spell," the witch warned. "True love. Do you understand?"

"Yes, Baba," Scarlett replied.

So she and Tomas did as the old witch instructed—they built a life. They built a cottage in the woods outside of Sevens, set the wards around it, and watched the hedge grow overnight. When her daughter was born filled with the magic of her father and mother, she and Tomas named her Jessamine. They tied her tiny wrist with the magical ribbon. They learned what it meant to love one another and lived as man and wife. Just as Baba predicted, she had been needed.

When Tarley was born, she took Scarlett's gift as a Prophet Augur, and Scarlett tied a red ribbon around her wrist. Then Brinna was born, taking Dream Walking and receiving her ribbon. Auri, Wisdom Oracle. Mattias, Time Runner.

Nearly twenty-eight years later, Scarlett now sat in the cottage where she'd made a life, her grown children—all but Jessamine—with their true loves, listening to the story.

Scarlett's secrets were revealed. Though the weight of carrying the burden of the truth should have lifted, it hadn't. Rather, the weight of shame and guilt came crashing down.

Tomas

Tomas Fareview, only son of Remison and Ginnet Fareview, husband of Scarlett and father of their children, watched the fire move in the hearth like a dancer. While he might have appreciated that at one time, at the moment he couldn't seem to feel anything but all-consuming hurt. It was a gloom that swallowed up everything inside him, a beast feeding on everything that had once made him feel whole. Now, he was just parts, and those parts were scattered and haphazardly existing without any semblance of being cohesive again.

He felt eviscerated.

He wished he had been. It might be easier to be lying out under the open sky with his guts dripping around him as he bled to death. Less painful.

Only as Scarlett—the object of his pain—finished telling her story to their children, that pain increased.

It wasn't as if he hadn't known her story. He had. She'd already been pregnant with Jessamine when they met. He'd been the tiny man traveling about the woods coercing people with his cleverness into helping him—a novelty, a joke, a trickster. He'd been whatever he needed to be. But the moment he'd met Scarlett, his purpose had shifted. He hadn't looked to serve himself, to coerce or trick for his own selfish needs, but rather to take care of her.

When she'd trusted him, she'd told him her story. Though she'd been named Azleah in another life, Scarlett was the only name he'd ever known. That was her true name to him. Scarlett, who'd looked at him like he was a giant rather than the tiny man no bigger than her thumb. Scarlett who'd loved him before the witch in the woods had reversed the spell making him a full-sized man he was now. Scarlett, who'd owned his heart long before then, but he hadn't ever considered that she would one day be his.

He'd never entertained the idea that a woman would ever love him. And even after meeting Scarlett certainly not a woman as lovely as her. He was content to be her friend, her helper. Being small had ensured his loneliness. Only

Scarlett made sure he wasn't alone. She had stayed. As time passed, he'd fallen in love with her, accepting it would be unrequited. Content to love her in secret, for who could ever love such a small man.

But then she'd confessed her feelings: *"I love him as he is."* That moment became his entire reason for his existence.

His love wasn't unrequited.

Scarlett loved him.

Of course he'd agreed to the witch-of-the-wood's plan to make him a full-sized man. To hide with his family. To love them. To protect them. To carry Scarlett's secrets to keep them all safe.

And he'd loved her with every fiber that made him whole. He loved her like a giant.

But she'd lied to him, and that, he wasn't sure he could forgive.

"What?" Auri breathed the question. "Jessamine's father?"

Tomas looked away from the blaze at Scarlett, who was staring at him once more with a pleading look in her eyes. He loved her eyes, those windows to her soul that reflected a stormy sky. But it hurt to look into them just then. She'd made a promise to tell the truth. Instead, she'd tricked them with the sleeping potion. She'd been willing to let them all sleep their lives away lost to the nightmares rather than tell them the truth.

"Crue. Yes," she said, telling the truth now when telling it risked nothing.

"Father?" Mattias's voice, then his hand on Tomas's shoulder grabbed his attention.

"What?" He tilted his head up to look at his son.

"Is this true?"

"Yes," he answered Mattias.

"And you knew?"

"Yes." He had. Every bit of it. Perhaps he was no better than Scarlett, keeping it from them, but he hadn't felt it was his story to tell. He'd known the consequences of telling it. He'd promised to help her keep them safe. And now Jessamine was gone.

He stood, turning to face his family. Mattias stood next to him, nearly even with his gaze now. Tarley and Lachlan, Auri, Brinna, the gods, and the soldier. "I knew. And I remained silent. And Jessamine may be... someone else's blood, but she is my daughter as much as each of you. I love her like I love each of you."

"You've been lying to us our whole lives." Tarley's anger was fair.

They weren't wrong. He knew he could have come up with a million excuses, but none exonerated him from holding onto Scarlett's lies.

Rather than say anything, he nodded.

Dropping the blanket from around his shoulders into the chair where he'd been sitting, he moved away from the fire, unable to keep the floating parts of himself contained. He wondered if he was on the verge of shrinking back down to the size of a thumb now that the spells had been broken. Perhaps becoming what he once was had always been his fate. He wasn't sure if it would be a sad relief to become as small physically as what he felt on the inside. Perhaps it would relieve the massive ache in his heart.

Grabbing his ax from next to the door, he walked from the cottage out into the woods, because at least there, his smallness felt right against the size of the trees.

Scarlett

Watching Tomas's broad shoulders disappear through the doorway crushed her. She stood, wanting to go after him but knowing she couldn't. Not yet. He needed his space, and she needed to finish what she'd started here. She'd finally revealed the truth, and they needed to find Jessamine.

"Don't blame him," she said. "I asked him to hold onto my secrets. And the secrets—not that I'm offering it as an excuse—were tied to the spells. Had I revealed any of them, the ribbons, the hedge would have failed."

"So you didn't trust us," Tarley snapped.

"I didn't trust Crue not to find us."

"Well, he found us anyway. Spells and all," Auri replied. "And now he has Jessamine."

Scarlett nodded. "He did. But your father... he asked me to tell you the truth for years."

"And you didn't," Brinna said.

"I didn't. I was afraid." She paused, wanting to explain herself but knowing that perhaps there was no way to appeal to them. The witch had warned her, and Scarlett hadn't listened. "I was afraid of Crue. His power. I was afraid of him hurting any of you, because of the magic–"

"What magic?" Mattias asked.

Scarlett pointed at Tarley, "Prophet Augur," then at Brinna, "Dream Walker," then to Auri, "Wisdom Oracle," and to Mattias, "Time Runner."

"You knew?" Brinna asked.

"Suspected. When you started dreaming, I realized the gifts had been transferred to each of you. It was just a matter of time to figure out who'd developed which gift."

"And Jessamine?"

"Healer," Lucian said, his hands on Brinna's shoulders. "She carries the godlight gift."

Scarlett nodded.

"Like you," Auri said.

"Yes. Like my mother before me." She paused, looking at the fire, wishing it were warming her. She just felt cold. "We have to find Jessamine. I don't know what he plans to do with her." Scarlett's heart stopped up in her chest, and tears flooded her eyes. "He once said he would consume her—us—for the magic."

"That's disgusting," Nixus said with a grimace.

Scarlett glanced from the god to Auri, whose head was tilted down. With one hand she clung to Brinna, and with the other she swiped her own tears.

"I don't know if it was literal," Scarlett said, "but I didn't have any reason to believe it wasn't."

"How do we find her?" Mattias asked.

"We wait," Lachlan said.

"What? We can't–" Scarlett started, tripping out of the blanket as she stood.

"We have to. We don't know where he took her, and Johesha—the captain of my guard—has gone after her. He'll be back when he has information. He'll also have a plan," Lachlan said. He turned to Jude and took the trinket the soldier had handed him. "In the meantime, you're promoted to captain in Johesha's absence."

"But, Your Highness–"

"No," Lachlan held up his hand to silence Jude. "Johesha handed the duty to you. I trust him—and you—completely. I need you to round up the camp and get them prepped to leave. Pick three soldiers you trust to leave behind."

Jude nodded and left.

"That's it?" Scarlett asked. "All we're going to do is wait?"

"Technically, we aren't waiting," Nixus said. "There's a man on it. He's a little cranky for my taste, but he seems pretty good at his job." He was leaning against the wall near the door where the soldier disappeared, then smirked at Lachlan, before his eyes flitted to Auri as if hoping for a reaction. He didn't get one.

"And what do you suggest we do while your soldier is on the job," Scarlett snapped.

"Prepare ourselves," Lucian suggested. "You've said his man is a powerful sorcerer. We'll need to have a handle on our own power."

"His name," Nixus said. "We'll need his true name."

Lucian spun to face his brother. "You remember?"

"I told you, I don't forget things."

"You have," Auri said, without looking at him.

Scarlett swallowed. "Why doesn't he remember?"

Nixus made a disgusted sound and stomped from the house, a trail of shadow following even as they stretched to reach for Auri.

"The god-yoke."

"What is that?" Scarlett asked.

Brinna stood. "It's when two godlights are bound. A recognition of their matched souls." She glanced at Lucian.

"But when those godlights are stretched thin with distance, it affects the pair," Lucian explained.

"Because of the spell?" Scarlett asked.

"I had to make a choice," Lucian said. "It was to lock away his memories or let him and Aurielle die. I chose the memories."

Scarlett's stomach rolled. "Die?" Her hand covered her mouth. She swallowed. "I didn't know–" She paused, turning away from Auri and another way she'd caused her children pain. "Will he remember?"

"I hope so," Lucian said. "With time. Maybe."

A house of cards.

Scarlett needed to see the witch.

She turned back to her family, resolved. "I think you're right," she told Lucian. "They need to be far from here. And they need to learn how to use the gifts. But I never learned, not truly. I tore through time and space with Mattias's gift just trying to get away. I never learned how to use it."

"Then how are we supposed to learn?" Mattias asked.

She didn't have an answer. She couldn't be sure she'd find the witch.

"You'll come to Sol," Lucian said. He looked at Brinna, who smiled at him shyly.

Scarlett's breath caught at the look in their exchange, at the bright light that swirled around them. "You too?"

Brinna's head whirled to look at her, her cheeks stained with a blush. She glanced at Auri, then down at her own lap. "Yes. We dreamed together."

"And how you were able to break the spell," Scarlett

finished.

"What's Sol?" Mattias asked.

"Sol is my godseat in Elcadia," Lucian said. "We should take everyone." He paused, measuring Brinna's reaction, then glancing around at everyone else. "It will be safe there, and we'll find someone to teach you how to use your magic."

"We're supposed to be in New Taras," Lachlan said, glancing at Tarley. "Supporting Queen Keyanna with her transition of power."

"We can transport Tarley in and out of Sol and New Taras," Luc offered. "There's room at Sol for everyone. Aurielle, you'll have to come. The god-yoke."

Auri nodded.

"And Elsewhere Doors," Brinna said. "They're these doors that lead to..."

Scarlett's attention drifted to observing the group, disconnected from it. Though a pall hung in the cottage, everyone began talking about new possibilities, about the magic, about how to use it to go after Jessamine. There was hope. Scarlett was confronted with the realization that the burden she'd been carrying for so long hadn't needed to be hers alone. The witch had said as much.

Then it hit her like a punch to her heart: she hadn't been alone. Tomas had carried the burden with her the whole time. She just hadn't seen it.

Tomas

With the cart unloaded and replaced in the barn, Tomas stood at the entrance to the cottage, unsure. His time in the woods, the physical exertion of chopping down trees in his path, of swinging the ax and sinking it into the wood, had been helpful in releasing some of his hurt and anger. He'd cut more wood than necessary, however, and couldn't waste it. So he'd returned for the cart, collected the wood, then stacked it under the lean-to outside the cottage, as it glowed from inside with a welcoming light. They wouldn't need wood for a while.

The thought stopped him.

It felt like the acceptance of a future.

And now he stood at the door, unsure about what to expect upon entering the home he'd shared with his family. Unsure about what he wanted, and if there was a future at all.

With a deep breath, he turned the doorknob and walked in. His boots stamped against the wooden floor, making a comforting noise he'd always liked. It reminded him of home. There weren't many places where his boots made that sound. He associated it with returning to Scarlett, because that's what he'd always done.

He hung his hat on the hook and set his ax next to the door, fortifying himself. When he turned, Scarlett waited in front of the table. She looked as beautiful as she always did. Her auburn hair was braided, the end of it draped over her shoulder and tied with a strip of fabric. She wore a dark blue dress. He'd always liked when she wore blue, and he was sure she knew it. The cottage was clean. Any vestiges of that last night before their sleep was cleared away. The table was set with two place settings. The fire was warm, candles glowed, and the scent of food cooking made his mouth water.

"Where is everyone?" he asked, afraid to know the answer.

"Gone," she answered.

His breath caught in his chest at the realization, a harsh

reality of the lies. He looked down at his feet, then sat to remove his boots like Scarlett liked. He paused, thinking maybe he wanted to stomp around in them, scatter dirt, but then discarded the thought just as quickly. He didn't want that at all. He just didn't want to hurt.

"Not forever," she added, quickly ascertaining the pain in his breath. "They'll return."

A breath of relief filled his lungs as he finished removing his boots. "They don't hate–"

"No!" She cut him off, and he looked up at her. She had that look of desperation he remembered from when they'd first met, her large eyes wide with fear, her features tense with uncertainty.

"They don't blame you," she said with a shake of her head. "The blame is where it should be."

"On Crue? Your father?" They'd been over that for years. He'd never blamed her for what had happened to her. Even now, he didn't begrudge her the truth of what brought her to him. It had brought her to him. His anger now was because she'd lied. She'd tricked them into consuming the sleeping potion rather than tell the truth, which he understood was related to her fear, but it highlighted a lack of trust in him, in their love, in their family. That was why it hurt so much.

She looked down at her hands clutched tightly in front of her, but didn't add anything. "Tarley and Lachlan are going to New Taras as planned."

"Is that why there's a flurry outside of the campsite across the way?"

"I assume. They'll return when we have news of Jessamine."

"We'll look then? For her?" Tomas walked across the room, passing Scarlett and the table to wash his hands at the sink. He pumped the water.

"We? Us?"

He heard the hope in her voice and picked up the bar of soap. "How else will we find her?"

"Lachlan's man. He thinks he'll return here–"

"To the cottage?"

"Yes. So he's leaving soldiers for when he does." She paused. "Mattias is going to go with Tarley."

Tomas swallowed the lump in his throat. "He always wanted to go to New Taras." He lathered the soap in his hands. Scarlett made it layered with citrus and lavender, and the scent made him think of her, always. Of that space on her neck just below her ear.

Scarlett hummed an affirmation.

He liked that sound. It made him think of when they kissed, when he touched her, tasted her. Annoyed with the direction of his thoughts, he smacked the bar of soap into the little dish near the sink and pumped clean water onto his hands, rinsing away the soap. Then he dried them with a clean cloth she'd left near the sink for that purpose. When he was done, he turned and leaned against the counter, his hands framing his hips. "Where's Mattias now?"

"With the girls. They've gone with the gods to Elcadia."

He harrumphed a sound. "That was always Auri's plan. Brinna too?" He couldn't bring himself to look at Scarlett, hesitant because he knew that the moment he did, staying angry would be difficult. He wanted to be angry. He wanted to rage and throw things. Then realized he had, with his ax. He'd burned a lot of his anger away, and now what he had left was unresolved hurt caused by the woman he adored.

He wasn't sure what to do with it.

It wasn't as if they never fought. They did. A lot. Scarlett was too stubborn for her own good most of the time. Usually when it came to their kids, hiding things, being unreasonably controlling, and Tomas trying to get her to be reasonable.

But now the truth was out.

And the cottage was empty for the first time in over twenty-seven years.

He finally raised his eyes to hers.

"I'm sorry," she whispered.

"Sorry for what?"

She took a deep breath. "For a lot of things, but mostly for not trusting you. I shouldn't have done this. I shouldn't have lied."

Tomas didn't move, frozen in place at her admission, though he shouldn't have been surprised. While she was extremely stubborn, she wasn't characteristically dishonest. Their squabbles were never around those kinds of things. They were always around her need to control.

The thought caught Tomas's breath.

Nearly twenty-eight years with this woman, he knew her. She hadn't lied to hurt him, not intentionally. She'd lied to keep control of a situation that was slipping out of her control. Tarley had married and planned to move away. Auri had announced she was leaving. Mattias was ready to venture out. For Brinna and Jessamine it was only a matter of time for the same. Without them contained, she couldn't keep them safe. And that—keeping them safe—had always been at the heart of their quarrels, the heart of Scarlett's motive: her needing to control things to keep them safe, and him wanting to loosen the reins.

But he was tired of begging her to let go. To let him take the lead.

"It's quiet," he said, suddenly unsure where they stood with one another. Everything that had once defined them was now stripped away. Though there was a new crisis—finding Jessamine—who they'd been together had been about averting it.

"I made dinner," she said, darting across the space. "It's ready."

"I'm not sure if I'm hungry," he said, though he was famished. He wasn't sure what he wanted. Wasn't sure if he could sit at a table worrying about Jessamine.

She stopped short. "Oh." Her face fell and Tomas hated that he'd done that.

It wasn't in his nature to hurt her. He'd spent his life trying to support her, so much so that this felt strange and unfamiliar. His first impulse was to backtrack, to appease, but he knew he couldn't, not for her, but for him.

"Okay." She was back to wringing her hands.

"I'm going to wash up. Since the girls don't need their room—I'll sleep there."

She nodded but didn't reply.

Tomas supposed there wasn't anything she could say. For the first time in their relationship, it felt as if he held the power, and it felt wrong somehow. He'd always thought of them as a team, until now. "I need some time," he added.

Scarlett swallowed but punctuated it with another nod. "I understand."

He pushed away from the sink and walked away, through the room they usually shared, though the doorway that led to a small vestibule where they often put the bathtub. Tomas didn't fill the tub. He pumped cold water and used it to wash away his dirt. Then, just like he said he would, he retreated up the stairs to the room his daughters had shared all these years and lay on his back staring up at the ceiling. It was the first time he could remember sleeping apart from Scarlett. Even when he'd been small, he'd curled up in the fabric of her clothes or in the softness of her hair.

What he knew was that he still loved her. He would always love that woman. The question was, would that love be enough for a future that felt so uncertain?

Scarlett

Without news and only her imagination to feed her worry, Scarlett was a mess. Not only was Jessamine missing, but the rest of her children were gone, and Tomas was distant, speaking in short, clipped sentences about nothing of substance. The next day passed in a blur of stops and starts, trying to find projects to keep her mind and hands occupied.

She'd started in the girls' room to make their beds, but the thought of what she'd done, of what they'd gone through, what they now faced, that she'd failed them, that they were gone, pulled her regret out in broken, unfettered sobs until she'd been unable to stay in the room.

She'd taken the sheets she'd stripped to wash and hang,

but as she pressed them into the water along the washboard, she found herself sinking into the memories of her youth until she felt like she was drowning.

She'd left the washing for the garden, where the soil and plants usually brought her balance. But as she'd sat amongst the herbs, the glaring absence of her daughters brought forth the fresh anguish of the truth.

Her children were gone. Jessamine was missing. She'd failed.

So she'd left for the kitchen.

When Tomas returned from the barn that afternoon, the sound of his boots on the floor captured her attention as she stood at the kitchen counter he'd made for her. His form in the doorway—wide and encompassing—was at first a buoying relief then a crushing disappointment.

She'd failed him.

He stalled, assessing, his eyes dragging along the countertop where she stood amidst a haphazard wreck of herbs—her supplies for making tinctures and medicines she took on calls and sold at the market.

"Did you mean to leave all your tools in the garden?" he asked. There wasn't any accusation in his tone, only curiosity. "And the laundry undone in the wash basin?"

When she didn't answer—because she couldn't seem to align the words with meaning—he asked, "What's going on here?"

Scarlett looked down at the mess she'd made, opened her mouth to tell him what she was doing, but her mind went blank. She couldn't remember what she'd been doing. She didn't know what she was doing anymore. The longer she looked at the greens, the pestle and mortar, the boiling pot, the less sense any of the disarray made.

"It's chaos, Scar," he said quietly next to her. "Unlike you."

She looked up from the mess to his face, to his kind eyes shaped with concern.

Scar. She'd always loved the way he shortened her name, the only one who ever did.

Then without warning, she burst into tears, pressing the towel in her hands against her face as her grief, pain, worry, regret, disappointment wrenched out of her with horrific gasp. She'd ruined everything.

Tomas gathered her into his arms with soothing sounds. "Hush," he whispered, his wide, heavy hand on the back of her head.

"I'm so sorry," she sobbed, grasping hold of his shirt, her face pressed into the strength of his chest.

He held her.

"They're gone," she sobbed. "I failed."

His arms squeezed her a touch tighter, and when his face pressed into the place between her neck and shoulder, Scarlett wrapped her arms around his neck, drawing up onto her toes, needing to be closer to his comfort.

"I failed too," he whispered, his lips against her skin. "We both have."

She shook her head. "Not you, Tomas." She drew back to look at him.

Raising his head, his eyes connected with hers, the sadness a deep, evergreen forest swirling inside them where he was lost. And it was her fault. She knew this. Had pushed him to go against his nature by keeping her secrets, securing the spells.

Unsure about anything but the tumult of emotions she couldn't seem to harness, Scarlett reached for comfort she knew he provided, a comfort she could reciprocate.

She kissed him, her hands framing his face, his beard soft against her palms.

He froze, tension tightening his shoulders.

And she thought he might pull away, but suddenly he was kissing her back, capitulating, needing, seeking. His tongue sought entrance, and she granted it. It was hungry, two souls on the periphery of starvation, finding one another in the darkness.

Groaning into that connection, Tomas growled and lifted her.

He was hard, and Scarlett tugged at her skirts between them, needing to feel him pressed against her core. "Please," she begged against his mouth. "I need you."

Tomas—still kissing her with relentless and punishing abandon—carried her across the space and put her on the cleared table, nipping at her lips with his teeth. She shoved forward with her own fiery answer to his angry kiss, needing, wanting the pain he might inflict. His discipline.

He growled and pushed her down onto her back.

Scarlett fought against the submission, coming back to tug at his suspenders, then fumbling with the buttons at his waist. "In need you in me, Tomas."

He shoved her skirt up, sliding his calloused palms up the thighs. When he reached her undergarment, he tugged them aside, and dipped his fingers inside her.

Crying out at the invasion, she grasped his shoulders.

"Already wet," he said, and circled her clit with his thumb.

Scarlett convulsed at the sensation tearing up her spine, mewling and moving her hips against the pressure. "Please."

With a roughness she'd never known from Tomas, he growled as he pulled his cock from his pants and gripped her hips, tugging her to the edge of the table, before pushing into her. She cried out, but he didn't check on her to see if he had hurt her like he might have in the past. Scarlett appreciated this taking. She ached. She wanted to hurt everywhere.

But Tomas didn't hurt her.

He never had. As Scarlett wrapped her legs around his

thrusting hips and dug her heels into his backside, she didn't feel hurt, she felt paradise, and didn't deserve this pleasure. She cried out with pleasure as Tomas pounded into her, but it turned to a sob that she tried to hide from him.

But Tomas never missed a thing.

He stilled, his chest heaving with exertion and need. With a frown, he grabbed her face and made her look at him. She knew what he'd see: tears streaming down her face. She knew that he'd misinterpret.

"I hurt you?"

She shook her head. "No. No."

But he was already withdrawing.

She scrambled off the table to her feet, grasping at his arms to keep him from buttoning up. To finish what they'd started. "Don't go."

His tortured eyes searched her face, emotions he'd never been able to hide playing out on his. "This was a bad idea. I shouldn't have–"

"Please. Tomas. No."

He shrugged back into his suspenders as he backed away. "I shouldn't have–"

"I asked you. I begged–"

But he held up a hand and shook his head. "I should be stronger when it comes to you," he said, and his throat bobbed. "This doesn't fix what's broken between us." Then he turned and left the cottage.

Scarlett watched him go, unsure how long she stood looking at the empty doorway before she burst into tears. She didn't know how to find a way forward.

Tomas

Inside the barn, Tomas ducked into Wilhemina's stall, his chest heaving with anguish at the thought he'd hurt his wife. The mare snuffed at him, looking for treats in his pockets, and Ferdie, the gelding, knickered on the other side of the stable wall as if he was missing out. Tomas wrapped his arms around the horse's neck and breathed deeply, drawing in her earthy scent to clear his head of Scarlett.

But he couldn't release what had happened between them, seeing it over and over in his mind. The frantic way he'd felt. The frenetic way she'd responded.

I hurt you?

She'd said no, but the tears...

His breath caught at what he'd done.

Never, in all his years as Scarlett's husband, had he ever been rough with her. He was so aware of his size, his strength. But just then, he'd found pleasure in dominating her. He'd never felt the need before, and it frightened him.

He'd learned to be a good lover to Scarlett. He'd asked her to teach him what she liked early on, and she had. She'd reciprocated, learning with him what he liked. They shared enjoyable intimacy and four of their own children to show for it, though in a small cottage filled with people, time together had been stolen and rarely exploratory. Never once, had he ever been so... forceful. Even now, in the aftermath, he felt the rush of it as if heated his cheeks and zipped down his spine with... longing. He swallowed and doused it with guilt.

She'd been crying.

And you left.

He'd never once left her. Not like that. The accusation and self-recrimination burned his chest. With his forehead against Wilhemina's neck, he pressed his hand against the ache. Even in spite of his hurt, he still loved Scarlett, and if what happened a few moments ago was any indication, still wanted her, needed her. Finding comfort in her body amidst the chaos of the rest of the emotions had felt... right.

He sighed, straightened, and dragged a hand over his face.

Wilhemina pushed up against his chest, huffing her frustration at his inattention.

"I didn't bring anything, girl," he whispered, running a hand down her neck.

She nuzzled him, switching her weight from one side to the other.

"Fine," he said and offered her and Ferdie some grain. Then he went back to work on repairing a bit of leather he used for hitching the horses to the cart.

When he'd worked through his chaotic thoughts, he knew he needed to find a way forward with Scarlett. He spent some time figuring out how to articulate it all, then returned to the cottage to talk to her. But as he walked in just before the sun sank below the horizon, Scarlett was tying on her cloak.

"What are you doing?" he asked.

"Going to the woods. There's some stew on the stove."

"At this time? That's not a good idea. Crue is still out there. The darkling."

"I can't wait. Sundown is the best time to find her."

"Who? Jessamine?"

She slipped on gloves. "Baba."

Frustration bubbled up inside him. "For fuck's sake, Scar. Haven't we had enough of magic," he snapped. "Look at where it's gotten us." He flew out a hand, indicating nothing, really, just the empty space of the cottage that felt like it was smothering them.

Her eyes narrowed. "I want to find Jessamine."

Stubborn woman.

"And I don't?" he retorted.

"That's not what I said."

He heaved a sigh, trying to reclaim that calm that usually ruled him. But since waking from the spell, it wasn't as easy. The dreams haunted him, so much so that even now, closing his eyes to sleep made his chest tighten with fear and despondency. But he gripped the feeling of calm, holding onto it tightly and said, "We should check in the village. See if anyone saw anything. We can go. Tomorrow."

She nodded. "Yes. And Baba might be able to–"

"Scarlett!" he shouted at her. "Stop! Listen to yourself! Was dosing your family with a sleeping potion not enough?"

"But if she can help–"

"Do you know who you sound like?" When she didn't ask for more, he told her anyway. "Your father."

Her mouth opened with shock.

"So one-track minded you can't see beyond the tip of your fucking nose."

"That's not–"

"It isn't? Maybe you haven't imprisoned anyone, but you're addicted to the magic and need it to keep control of everything around you, even to the detriment of those you love."

"That's not–"

He grasped the back of his neck and turned his back to her, reason and calm fleeing. "You've never listened to me," he said, more a lamentation than accusation.

"Tomas, that's not–"

He spun back to her. "Was it pity? Is that why you've stayed with me? Because you felt sorry for me?"

"No. No!" She shook her head. "I love you."

He shook his head and waved a hand. "I'm not sure this is love, Scar." He huffed, the anger a beast writhing and alive inside him, then waved a hand. "Do what you're going to do. I just..." He stopped and shook his head again. "It's your life."

"No. It's ours," she replied, reaching for him.

He stepped away from her touch. "Is it? Has it ever been?"

He waited for her to respond, but when she didn't—her face slack with surprise—he walked past her, through the house to the back room where he usually took his bath. Rather than bathe, however, he stood there breathing like he'd raced home through the woods, his eyes burning with the horrible awareness that his life had always been hers, and now he didn't know who he truly was either way.

Scarlett

Scarlett stomped out into the blue twilight as night fell, anger and hurt fueling her steps. Incredulity and justification inspired her forward. How could Tomas accuse her of being like her father? The king had trapped her in a tower, and in his madness, planned on making her his wife.

You trapped your family in a spell.

She stumbled, catching herself against the barn wall, her breath suddenly coming in gasps. No. No. It wasn't the same. She was trying to protect them.

You trapped your family in a spell.

Tomas's words lurched through her: *Just like your*

father. Was it pity? The reason you stayed with me?

A sob bubbled up from the depth of her soul as she sank down to her knees on to the cold ground. Leaning against the barn wall, forehead pressed against the wood-plank siding, she cried. She loved Tomas, absolutely loved him. She tugged at her coat in her grief, the breeze in the trees—a hollow whirl rustling the boughs of evergreens—the hum of the River Grimz in the distance, and the crickets somewhere chirping in the night mingling with her thoughts and tears.

"You were right," she sobbed out loud to the old witch, even though she was just outside the cottage and knew the old woman wouldn't hear her.

Baba had told her she would lose everything, and that was exactly what was coming to fruition. Scarlett had been so focused on her need to keep them safe, she'd ignored the warning.

Tomas had told her to tell their children. She hadn't listened.

Obsessed, just like her father.

She nearly gagged at the realization, wanting to deny it but couldn't. She had imprisoned her family in a spell, and though her intentions had been to keep them safe, it wasn't a far cry different from what her own father had done to *keep her safe.*

When the weeping subsided, the power of that pain waning, she sniffed and sat back onto her heels, still kneeling in the ground outside the barn.

Her first impulse was to get to her feet and stomp into the woods to demand answers from Baba, but then she turned to look at the cottage, the windows dark but for the single window upstairs where she knew Tomas was.

Has it ever been our life? he'd asked.

The thought grabbed hold of the air in her lungs, and she gasped, trying to draw a breath, looking back at the barn wall. Had it? Every choice, every decision she'd made since running from her father, from Crue, had been to hide them, keep them safe. She had relied on the witch and the magic to do it. They were living in the cottage amid the Whitling Woods for that very reason.

Tomas was right.

She glanced at the glowing window like a beacon in the darkness once more.

Tomas.

When she walked into the main room of the cottage, depleted of indignation and the lies she'd been telling herself, it was dark and cold. The fire had gone out. She removed her cloak and hung it on the hook Tomas had installed for her, then shuffled through the front room to the back, noticing each and every spot had been touched by Tomas in some way. The table he'd built. The kitchen he'd changed. The stove he repaired. Every bit of this cottage was a home he'd built for her. For them.

She was struck with an understanding so deep it barely rose to the consciousness of her mind, only in fragments coalescing rather than the whole picture that might overwhelm her though the essence of the truth was there. While she'd been living to protect them from Crue, Tomas had been living for her, for their family.

This isn't love.

Her knees nearly buckled, and she grabbed the wall at the bottom of the stairs to keep her upright as tears burned through her body once more. These weren't heavy sobs, but quiet tears laced with regret and shame.

She did love Tomas. She needed him to know that.

When the wave of tears passed, she wiped her face and looked up the dark stairwell to a faint glow seeping under the door at the top. Speaking to Tomas was paramount, so she climbed the stairs, the wood creaking with her steps, hoping that it wasn't too late to find a different path forward, to tell him she wanted to be different.

But when she was a few steps from the top, the light went out, casting everything in darkness and shadow.

Her throat tightened at the thought that perhaps she'd crossed the point of no return with him.

So she retreated.

When she reached the room she'd shared with him for the last twenty-eight years, her heart dipped into her belly and burned with anguish. Though they were in the same house, she felt alone. She wanted to stomp back up the stairs and rage at him, tell him where he belonged, but the indignation died in the truth of what she'd done fueling her guilt. He'd said he doubted that she loved him. That was her fault.

She stripped off her dress and garments and slipped into the bed to spend another night alone.

Then another.

Followed by another.

Tomas never returned to their bed at night and spent the days avoiding her. He was gone before her, and silent and sullen, retreating out into the barn or up into the attic room.

But he'd asked for time, so she gave it. For the next two weeks, she lay in their bed missing him. Missing his large body curled around hers, the safety of being in his arms. Missing the feel of his calloused hands on her body. Missing his kiss. Missing the way it felt when his body invaded hers, filling her. Besides the birth of the children, they'd never gone this long without one another before. And while sleeping without him was horrible, the longer the time stretched, the more restless her sleep turned, her dreams brimming with dark imagery.

And worse yet, in that time there was no word from Crue or Lachlan's man about Jessamine.

One morning, Scarlett woke up with a start just before

the sun rose and lay there trying to catch her breath as the dream overran her thoughts. Dark flowers were blooming and taking over everything in her garden. It didn't matter how much she yanked and pulled, they squeezed out all that was good. When she looked closer, the healthy plants had the faces of her family. By the time it drifted away, she got up and slid into a chemise, then shuffled through the door into the kitchen to start the fire and put on the water for coffee.

To her surprise, Tomas was in the kitchen, pumping out water from the sink, his pants hanging at his waist, suspenders draped over his hips and his mouthwatering torso bare.

"Oh," she said, pulling up short at the sight of him.

He turned and looked at her, his eyes skimming over her nightshirt, his gaze heating before he looked back to his task.

Scarlett glanced at the potbelly stove and noticed the crackle of a fire alive with heat and fuel. "You lit the fire."

He grunted and turned, holding a full kettle.

"Thank you," she said, recognizing he had always lit the fire, in more ways than one.

His eyes jumped to hers as he crossed the space to set the water on the stove, but he didn't say anything, just offered her a nod.

"About the other night," she said, taking a step toward him.

"Scarlett." He held up his hands and took a step away. "I can't."

"Can't what?" she asked, afraid to know what that meant.

"I can't do this right now," he said and started across the room.

"But we need to–" Scarlett started, only to be interrupted by a knock at the door. Her gaze bounced from the door back to Tomas, who'd stopped.

Her heart skipped, tripped, then raced.

"Are you expecting someone?" he asked.

She shook her head. They both knew Jessamine wouldn't knock. "Maybe it's news?" She walked over to the couch, pulling a blanket draped over the back, and throwing it around her shoulders like a shawl.

Tomas shrugged into the shirt he'd dropped on the table, then stopped at the threshold of the closed door. "Who is it?" he asked.

"Trevis, sir. Come to fetch Miss Scarlett for Mimi."

A deflated sigh filled with possibility left her, and tears cut the back of her eyes.

Tomas glanced over his shoulder at her, then opened the door to the boy who worked at the stables of the Copper Pot Inn. He swung his overgrown blond hair from his eyes and flashed a brilliant smile unaware that anything was amiss.

"Mimi is in labor?" Scarlett asked him.

He nodded. "Credence sent me."

"Let me get my things," she said and started back to the room to dress.

"What happened to the hedge?" she heard the boy ask as she shut the door. Tomas's deep voice rumbled as he answered.

With a sigh, she pushed away from the door disappointed that she couldn't have this conversation with Tomas now, but perhaps some more time was best for him. Here the universe was offering it.

When she came back out into the main room of the cottage, Tomas was still there waiting with Trevis, surprising her. Both of their faces turned when she opened the door.

"Ready then," she said and though she said it to Trevis, her eyes sought Tomas.

Her husband scratched at his brown beard he always kept neat but looked like it needed a trim. He glanced at her for a moment and ran a hand through his brown hair. Like his beard, it was a touch too long, curling around his face. She was the one who usually trimmed it, but he hadn't asked. "Well then," he said.

She wanted to scream but just ground her teeth together and met them both at the doorway. Living like this was going to tear her apart, she decided. Living their lives together but separated wasn't going to work. Though she was trying to be patient and give him the time he needed, neither of them deserved to live in this purgatory.

Without looking at him, she said, "It could be a couple of days. Mimi's first baby."

"Alright," he said quietly and nodded, his eyes on the floor between her feet.

She wanted more, but he wasn't going to provide it. So she started through the door, but Tomas stopped her, a strong hand wrapped around her arm. She looked up at him.

"Is it safe?" he asked quietly, his eyes bouncing to Trevis, who had wandered out into the yard, then back to her.

Scarlett wanted to imbue those words with hope, but it struggled to stay afloat. "Does it matter?" she asked but didn't wait for Tomas to reply, leaving the cottage behind but taking her heartbreak with her.

# Tomas

'*Does it matter?*'

Scarlett's question plagued him the whole of the day after she left for Sevens. He knew where she was: the skinhouse. Mimi was a worker that Scarlett had been monitoring since the young woman had learned she was pregnant.

Even knowing where Scarlett was, watching her walk away ate at him.

Everything ate at him.

He'd left for the forest to collect wood to repair the lean-to and firewood for a few of the merchants in Sevens. The giant trees rose up around him, and he felt judged. Since his fight with Scarlett about the witch, he'd taken the distance he'd asked for. While he'd hoped it would offer him clarity, maybe even provide him direction, it only served to make him long for his wife. That was confusing, considering all she'd done.

And yet, he understood it.

She'd been abused, lied to, threatened, tricked, chased. She'd always needed to control the outcome of things, hadn't ever lied to him about wanting to be a better parent than her own—to protect her children. While he knew his understanding didn't excuse her choice, it helped his hurt and anger fade some.

The truth was that Scarlett had fallen in love with him before he had been a full-sized man. She'd extended grace to choose him regardless of his size. It had been the witch who'd given him that gift. If anyone understood the lure, the call, and the danger of magic, it was him. Considering all the ways Scarlett had been hurt and how magic had been the only means to protect herself, perhaps it hadn't been fair of him to be surprised that's where she defaulted to find Jessamine.

Did it matter?

When she didn't return that night, Tomas sat in the cottage watching the fire and wondering what to do. His heart and mind were wild with worry, but he resisted the urge to saddle Ferdie and visit the skinhouse to make sure

Scarlett was safe. While he didn't chase the impulse, it offered him some truths. First, that he cared about Scarlett and her safety and second—that wildness inside him was more than just concern.

He pictured her walking into the kitchen that morning in her nightshirt, her hair mussed with sleep, knowing she'd been bare underneath. It was how she always slept. His innards had tilted, his equilibrium unbalanced at the way he missed her. Sleeping apart had become a burden, and though he thought it was what was best to get a clear sense of the path forward, each night away from her had become harder and harder to bear. The time was ripping the hole in his chest bigger and wider. Being stuck in the uncertainty of in between was no way to live.

He wanted his wife as much now as he had twenty-eight years ago.

He cared for Scarlett's well-being.

The truth was, he loved her. He'd never stopped.

So yes, it fucking mattered.

She'd tried to talk to him, and he'd been the ass to rebuff her attempt.

As soon as she returned, he decided. They would talk.

The following day, he stayed close to home, hopeful for her return. But as he chopped wood and stacked it in the cart, she didn't appear in the lane.

She still didn't return after he'd finished lunch. His

anxiety spiked at thoughts that she was in danger, that Crue had found her and stolen her away.

By the time Tomas finished with firewood orders, he couldn't contain himself—he saddled Ferdie and raced into Sevens, his mind racing as the gelding galloped toward town.

He hitched Ferdie to the post outside the skinhouse. He wasn't completely comfortable going in, never having visited before, but his need to know Scarlett was safe overrode any discomfort. He turned the doorknob and entered.

It was nice. A comfortable entry, tastefully decorated, though he wasn't sure what he would have expected, not having any experience about it either way. In his first twenty-two years, he'd met one woman who'd sold her body—Glinda had been her name. Tomas had hitched a ride on her shoulder, and while Glinda had hinted at the struggle to survive which necessitated her profession, she'd been a kind, funny, and accommodating companion.

"Mr. Fareview!" The proprietress of the establishment smiled when she looked up from the settee in the entry. "I didn't think I would ever see you here." Stella laughed as if she'd made a good joke. "I assume you're here for Scarlett."

He didn't answer, just nodded tightly at her, his eyes skimming the long hallway, the stairwell, the bar area. "She's okay?"

Stella's smile widened. "I'd expect she's exhausted. Baby is taking its time, and poor Mimi is having a rough go of it being her first babe and all. Would you like me to get her?"

Tomas shook his head and backed away. "No. Don't want to interrupt. Just checking on her."

Stella's brown eyes twinkled.

He nodded his head though nothing had been said and withdrew from the building, looking up at it once he was outside, his heart racing with... trepidation? Fear? He wasn't sure. He knew where Scarlett was, so why did he feel so unsettled?

Instead of returning to the cottage, he retreated to the Copper Pot and bellied up to the bar, where Horance poured him an ale.

"Everything alright, Tomas?" Horance asked, wiping his hands on a cloth. Horance's bulk blocked much of the view of the tapped kegs were lined up along the wall. Tomas hadn't met many men as big as he was, but Horance was close.

Tomas nodded. "Fine."

Since Horance wasn't a man of many words and neither was Tomas, they existed in companionable silence as he finished his ale. He still didn't return to the cottage, staying to have another ale, and then another. As he drank, he meandered his memories and realized he'd spent most of his first twenty-two years alone. Sure, he'd grown up with his parents, who he'd left when he'd turned fourteen. Then he'd done what he could to get by, relying on cleverness and charm to make his way in a giant world.

But those interactions had always been transactional. He'd never had anyone to call home. Until Scarlett. So going back to an empty cottage wasn't what he wanted, and he was beginning to suspect it wasn't what he needed either.

Scarlett

The baby howled his first cry shortly before dawn on the third day. Though Scarlett had known Mimi's birth would take some time, she didn't understand why she was feeling the way she was about it. But as she reflected further, she realized it was because things were so uncertain with Tomas. It made her nostalgic for when everything seemed so clear when their children were young. She'd left things with Tomas unresolved, and it didn't feel right.

After making sure Mimi and the baby were tucked up and surrounded by people who loved them, she descended to the lobby, ready to go home.

Stella stood, wrapped in a robe, waiting, and handed

Scarlett the promised luri. "Thank you, Scarlett. I don't know what we'd do without you."

"Find a way," Scarlett said, wondering what she would do if Tomas decided that he no longer wanted to remain partners. Though she had a trade to support her, life without him felt bleak. She would find a way too, she supposed.

"By the way," Stella said, "that husband of yours is a treasure."

The mention of Tomas stopped her. "Excuse me?" Scarlett knew that to be true but tilted her head at Stella, who read the question in Scarlett's gaze.

"He was here last night."

"He was?" Her heart bounced inside her chest. "Did he say why?"

"Just came to check on you." Stella tightened her robe. "Didn't say much but wanted to make sure you were safe, I'd guess." Stella smiled. "Keep that one close. Not very often a good one comes along."

Scarlett nodded. "Oh. Yes. A good one," she mumbled, dumbfounded, and backed out beyond the front door, her mind tripping over why Tomas might've come. He'd known where she was, what she was doing. Maybe there was news.

She whirled around, to find Tomas standing in the middle of the road, leaning against Ferdie. Her heart stopped. Then it raced. He looked as he usually did. His dark boots crossed at the ankle, muscular legs filling dark trousers held up by suspenders, though she knew he didn't truly need them. His broad chest and shoulders were covered with an ivory tunic she'd made him, and though there was chill in the air, he hadn't worn a jacket, his sleeves rolled to his elbows, his strong arms on display. His head was tipped down, his chin to his chest as if he were asleep, leaning up against Ferdie.

Tentative hope and light burst inside her chest as she took a step toward him.

Then he looked up, and when he saw her, he straightened. Ferdie side-stepped at the loss of Tomas's weight, the animal obviously leaning into him as well.

"You're here," she said.

He grunted, stepped forward, and took the bag from her hand. "Yeah," was his reply.

She was bursting with the need to ask him all the questions on her mind but was afraid to break the spell that wove its way between them—its own kind of magic. So she didn't say anything, just waited, giving Tomas the lead.

"Thought you might be tired." He set down her satchel at Ferdie's feet, then turned and held out his hand.

Scarlett took it and stepped toward him. "Yes. Thank you. Have you been waiting long?"

Tomas captured her waist in his hands and lifted her

onto the gelding's back, his hands lingering a moment before he bent to retrieve her bag and handed it off.

"Spent the night at the inn." He climbed up onto the horse behind her, then adjusted to accommodate the both of them, settling her a touch closer between his spread thighs, her legs draped over one of his. Nestling her body safely between his arms, he clicked his tongue, flicked the reins, and turned Ferdie around.

"The inn?" Scarlett asked as the Ferdie clomped through Sevens.

"Drank a little too much with Horance."

"Horance drank?"

"No. He just served me and laughed at me when I could barely stand."

"You drank?"

He hummed an affirmation. "Let me sleep it off there."

The sun was just hinting at the horizon, the sky above the sharp treetops a thin blue touched with streaks of pink, orange, and yellow. There wasn't a cloud in the sky—strange for Sevens—but it was going to be a beautiful fall day. It was so early, the thoroughfare was empty but for the sound of Ferdie's hooves hitting the packed earth.

Scarlett rifled through her bag for an herbal candy she'd made for the effects of a hangover. "This might help," she said and held up the sweet drop in her hand.

Tomas's eye dipped to her open hand, but instead of

grabbing it, his eyes jumped up to hers, and he opened his mouth, his command clear.

Scarlett swallowed but lifted the drop to his lips, her gaze trailing the movement of her hand to his mouth. His lips closed around her fingers, his tongue caressing her skin as it curled around the sweet drop. Her heart quickened in her chest, a shimmer of a dance filled with buoyancy, and she looked up at Tomas whose gaze was filled with heat.

Scarlett didn't speak, afraid to, but looked to the lane ahead of them as she relaxed against Tomas's chest.

He didn't speak either until they'd turned onto the lane toward the cottage. "How did she do?"

"Mimi?" When he grunted, she answered, "A rough go. Got a little worried, but she made it through."

"She had you," he said.

She turned her head to look at him, moved by the pride she heard in his voice. "Stella said you came."

He grunted again in acknowledgement, his cheeks tinted with a blush.

Scarlett looked back at the road ahead and pondered this information. Tomas had come to the skinhouse to check on her, he'd ended up at the pub and drank so much he couldn't get home—uncharacteristic of her husband—then he'd waited for her, and now he blushed that she knew. She nestled closer into him, going so far as to lean her head against his chest—partially to test if he'd allow it, partially because she was so tired, and mostly because she needed him.

He did allow it, one of his arms wrapping around her, to hold her steady. "Rest," he said.

She needed to, but her mind was buzzing with all the things they needed to talk about. There so much she wanted to say.

But she realized Tomas wasn't a man of words. He was a man of action.

Her words died before they were said as she realized she needed to show him, prove she wanted a way forward between them. So she just rested her head against him, listening to his steady heartbeat.

A little while later, Tomas hummed a happy noise that reverberated through his chest and into Scarlett, and Ferdie nickered, huffing excitedly. "Scar?" he said quietly.

She sat up and looked at him before turning to see what he was smiling at. Standing at the door of the cottage were Brinna and Auri, Lucian with them.

"Hello!" Tomas called as he brought Ferdie to a stop and dismounted, helping Scarlett down from the horse to the ground. His face was beaming with delight, but anxiety gripped Scarlett.

She bit her tongue from asking if there was news, and shut her eyes, resetting. Choosing forward met being more patient, she decided. When she opened her eyes, Tomas was watching her.

"Morning, Father." Brinna curled up into her father's embrace, then made way for Auri, who did the same. "Mother," she said.

Scarlett looked at Lucian, still by the steps to the doorway. He looked hesitant to leave. "Afraid I've got another spell up my sleeve?" she asked.

His eyes narrowed. "Truthfully, Scarlett. Yes."

"Fair enough," she answered.

Neither of her daughters embraced her.

"I'll help you with Ferdie," Auri told Tomas, never meeting Scarlett's gaze. "I'd like to see Wilhemina too."

Scarlett watched Auri and Tomas walk toward the barn, then turned to Brinna and Lucian. "You're here early." She led them into the cottage.

"You were on a call?" Brinna asked, her eyes dropping to Scarlett's satchel.

"Mimi Wills had her baby."

Brinna smiled and glanced at Lucian, then blushed. "We just came to check on you. See if perhaps Lachlan's guard had returned."

The hope that had started with the sunrise remained as Scarlett set the satchel on the table then moved to get a fire going in the hearth. "We haven't. I'd hoped perhaps you had news." She stuffed the tinder in the kindling.

"No. But Lucian's sister—Lexa—thinks she knows

someone to help us learn how to use the magic," Brinna said.

"Tarley and Mattias, too?" Scarlett lit the tinder and leaned forward, blowing on it before looking at Brinna when it caught.

Brinna nodded. "Yes."

"They're... alright? You're all alright?" She swiped at her dress swallowed the guilt and rose up inside her.

Brinna frowned and glanced at Lucian, who was also frowning. "No, Mother. We're not. Auri and Nix most of all."

She nodded, knowing now that she'd planted a terrible harvest, and this was what it was reaping. "I didn't know."

No one said anything. What was there to say to that, really?

Scarlett moved back to the table, trying to do something with her nerves, spending the energy on something rather than standing idly waiting for the next words that Brinna might say that would deflate her hope further. Grabbing her satchel, she began organizing its innards, pulling emptied containers to discern what she needed to refill and make more of.

"Mother?"

She stopped and looked at Brinna, waiting, unwilling to offer up any more words that might increase the distance between her and her daughter.

"How are you?"

That hadn't been what she expected. Tears filled her eyes until Brinna blurred before her. Before Scarlett could catch them, several slipped down her cheeks. "What?" was all she could push past her thick throat. Then she whirled back to the fire and added several chunks of wood.

Suddenly Brinna, her sweet, sweet Brinna, grabbed hold of Scarlett and helped her into a chair at the table. "Sit." Brinna pulled a chair so she was facing Scarlett, so close their knees were nearly touching. Then she gathered Scarlett's hands between her palms.

"I saw your dreams," Brinna said. "During the spell. And Lucian" –she glanced over her shoulder to look at the golden god, watching the exchange from several feet away before looking back at Scarlett– "saw..."

Brinna stopped and swallowed, looking down at her lap and shaking her head as if to dispel whatever she saw in her mind's eye.

"I uncovered your story," Lucian said simply.

Brinna lifted her eyes filled to the brim with emotion and nodded. Tears slipped down her cheeks.

Suddenly, their reaction after the spell had been broken made sense. Their understanding.

Scarlett wasn't sure how she felt about that, having wanted to protect her children from that awful truth. She would have taken it to her grave if it had been possible to save them from the horrible awareness. But now the truth was theirs too.

There were parts she was ashamed of—like falling prey to Crue—but now, nearly twenty-eight years later, she recognized she'd always been the victim and shouldn't carry the blame, even if knowing it didn't always reconcile with living it.

More tears slipped from her eyes. "I just wanted to protect you from it. From him."

Brinna squeezed her hands. "Only now, you don't need to anymore. Now we just need to focus on getting Jessamine back."

Scarlett's eyes flashed to Lucian, then back to Brinna. "I've ruined everything," she whispered.

Brinna glanced over her shoulder and offered the god a teary smile. "I think Lucian has some wisdom he could share about that."

The golden god smiled at Brinna, a brilliant look filled with love and adoration. He closed the space until he was sitting at the table next to Brinna, wrapping a hand around the back of her neck. "The story starts with a young god named Nixus and his villainous older twin brother, Lucian." His gaze jumped to Scarlett. "Thinking I was doing the right thing at the time, I cast a spell that trapped him for over ten years. He almost didn't make it out but for a plucky key keykeeper named–" He stopped and looked at Brinna expectantly.

Brinna smiled, bumping against him with her back. "Aurielle Fareview."

Chills raced across Scarlett's skin. "Auri?"

"The Great Nap Escapade," Brinna clarified.

Scarlett's eyes jumped between Brinna and Lucian. "The key she wears?"

Lucian nodded. "That is where she and Nixus met, where they were god-yoked. The spell was my fault, you see."

Scarlett disconnected from Brinna's hold and covered her mouth with a hand.

"I understand regretting a choice," Lucian said, "but someone taught me that you can't get stuck there." He cleared his throat and glanced at Brinna, who nodded. "I saw your father," he added.

Scarlett jumped up, her chair hitting the floor with a loud bang. "How?"

Lucian held out his hands. "Clarification. He's in the Netherrealm, long dead from the world. He can't hurt you."

She nodded even though her heart raced, and she shook with the need to flee.

"He was stuck even in the afterlife, a husk, I'm sure, of the good man he'd once been, but fighting with all the versions of the man he'd become. Stuck in his mind and his obsession with your mother."

Scarlett nodded, her stomach swirling with nausea, her

hand still pressed against her mouth.

"And I tell you this to say that the choice you made, the choice I made—albeit terrible ones—don't have to keep us stuck. We can make other choices, better ones. Ones that heal and grow."

The dark flowers in Scarlett's dream surfaced in her mind.

"I forgive you, Mother," Brinna said, "and I understand why, even if I don't agree."

A sob rasped and caught in Scarlett's throat. She covered her face with her hands, unable to hold back. When Brinna's arms wrapped around her, Scarlett leaned into her child, finally understanding what Tomas had been telling her all along.

Tomas

"Are you alright?" Tomas asked Auri as they walked into the barn, leading Ferdie behind them. "Is it nice where you are? Safe?"

Auri glanced at him. "I should be asking you that."

"Why?"

"Because you're stuck here with her."

"Auri–"

She huffed a breath. "I'm sorry. I am. I'm just so angry."

"Go get me the brush," he said and watched Auri walk across the barn. She stopped to give Wilhemina some affection, and he led Ferdie into the paddock.

"Good boy," he hummed and patted the gelding, unbuckling the saddle and pulling it from the horse's body along with the blanket to drape them over the railing.

"Your anger is justified," he said. "For both of us."

Auri appeared in the doorway, then shut the gate behind her. "You?"

"I kept her secrets, Auri. From you. From you all."

"Why doesn't that feel as bad?"

He shrugged.

Aurielle sighed. "I knew something was up, right away. Nixus–" Her voice caught, and she swallowed which made Tomas unsure and unsteady for her.

Using the brush on Ferdie's fur, Auri appeared to reset, her features softening. "Anyway, Nix told me there was more to the story, and he was right. And I just knew, every time Mother would say something, that it wasn't the whole of it. It's that power, this knowing, like she said." Auri held her hands out in front of her, and though they were empty, it was like she could see what lay in her palms, the brush included. "I can see all these puzzle pieces in my head and when one is missing or one is more important, it stands out."

Tomas took the brush from Auri and smoothed Ferdie's other side with the thick bristles.

"Yes. We're safe," she said, finally answering his initial question. "Lucian's home is beautiful. And Lexa, that's Nix and Lucian's sister, knows someone to help us with the magic."

Tomas frowned, handing the brush back to Auri, hating the magic for no other reason than what it had wrought on his family.

"I remember Lexa," he said, recalling her from the meadow where she'd descended as a dragon. He removed the bridle, unbuckling the harness from the horse's head and drawing the bit from Ferdie's mouth. "A good thing?" He rubbed the gelding's velvet nose.

"If it can help us get Jessamine back, I think so."

He nodded, and they finished up with Ferdie. Auri gave him grain and feed while Tomas put the tack away. When he re-emerged from the tack room, Auri was standing at Wilhemina's paddock, speaking softly to the mare.

"Your mother," he said, surprised he'd started that way, but the conviction to still support Scarlett was heavy on his heart.

Auri looked up. "I know the story."

"Knowing the story and understanding the story are two different things. Like your power. You might have it, know it's there, but being able to use it requires a deeper understanding."

She swallowed, nodded, and pressed her forehead to Wilhemina, a position he found himself in a lot.

"I met her just after she escaped the tower." He paused, leaning against the wall across from his daughter. Looking at the floor, he tracked the grain of the wood near her feet, trying to find the reason he was speaking about this at all, unsure where his memories were taking them. They felt important somehow, whether it was for Auri or him, he didn't know.

"She was so afraid," he continued. "I'll never forget that." He frowned remembering that visceral fear on her face. "I'd been a selfish prick up to that point in my life. Really only cognizant of myself and my own needs, and this beautiful woman dropped into my world—literally—and needed me. I felt seven feet tall."

"You are nearly seven feet tall," Auri quipped.

Tomas offered her a short smile. "That's the thing about your mother. She never made me feel small, even when I could fit in the palm of her hand. She never looked at me like I was less than."

Even if her actions had of late —but he could see it had been an act born of her desperation, and Scarlett backed into a corner was a feral creature. He'd been the one to see himself as small. That wasn't her fault.

"Why are you telling me this, Father?"

Tomas sighed. "Things change," he said quietly, more to himself than to her.

She looked a bit taken aback by the statement. "What does that mean?"

He looked up at his daughter. "Things can't remain unchanged. I changed when I met your mother. I wanted to be better for her. Now she's changing. Our whole family is changing. It's the law of living, I suppose."

Auri was quiet.

The horses snuffed and nickered, wanting attention.

"Do you still love her?" Auri asked.

"Yes," he said without hesitation. "That is one thing that remains unchanged, but love evolves, I think, as we do."

"Right," Auri said, pressing a hand to her heart. "I'll have to try."

Tomas didn't understand what she meant by her words—not completely—but it connected to his heart somehow, the final missing piece of a puzzle dropping into place.

Scarlett

After Auri, Brinna and Lucian left, Tomas's eyes found hers.

"I'll be heading into the village tomorrow," he said. "Ask around about Jessamine. I'm tired of waiting."

She nodded. "Okay. I'll be ready."

He nodded, then walked away.

"Tomas?" she called.

He stopped and turned back toward her.

"Should we talk? About us?"

"Yes," he said, backing away. "I just need to get my thoughts in order." He disappeared once more up the stairs.

Scarlett watched him go, wanting to push him into

doing it now. But it was his turn to lead them, so she didn't and spent another restless night without him.

The lack of hedge was still strange as they set off the next morning. The safety of it had been part of their existence as long as they'd lived in Sevens. That protective fence had offered her security, and now that it was stripped away, she was exposed.

"Do you think Crue will look for us?" Tomas asked as they started down the road toward side by side.

Scarlett hummed a response, more to give herself time than as an actual answer. She didn't want to talk to Tomas about Crue, but finding Crue was how they would find Jessamine. "No. He has what he wants."

"Not everything," he said, glancing at her.

"He has Jessamine."

"Do you think he'll..."

"Consume her?" Her voice shook as she said it, unsure how to answer and unable to offer any more solace than she could provide herself. "I don't know what he'll do."

They walked in silence for longer than was comfortable. "Tomas–"

"We need to–" he started at the same time. "Sorry," he said. "You first."

"I do love you," she said, unwilling to allow him any more time to think that wasn't so.

"Why did you lie to me?"

"I didn't tell you about the potion because I knew you would disagree and you'd fight me on it."

"So you just don't trust me?"

"I do."

"Just not enough to also have our children's best interest at heart? Or yours? Ours?"

Her eyes burned with tears hearing his words. She could see his point, and while it was fair, she wasn't sure how to reconcile her choice with his needs. It was a fair question. "I do trust you, I didn't want to take the risk–"

"–which still led to Jessamine being taken by Crue."

"Yes," she bit out. "Had I considered that..."

"If you'd asked me, you might have."

The bitterness was evident in his voice, and it made Scarlett feel defensive. "I just did what I thought was right."

"But that's always the case, isn't it, Scarlett. It's always what you think is right. Your decision, your plans, your way or no way."

She bristled against his observation, wanting to deny it, but she'd damned herself. She had nothing to hold her up. "I was just trying to protect them." And failed.

They walked in silence, Scarlett pondering what he'd said and hating how it convicted her, hating that she knew he was right. She'd made it easier for Crue to get his hands on Jessamine. Her fault. And the sensation of having alienated Tomas was a rendering of what made her whole.

"Why do you think he only took Jessamine?" she asked.

"As opposed to both of you?"

"Why leave at all?" she asked. "He made it through the hedge. Got to us."

They walked in silence, her mind working it over. What she knew of Crue was that he wanted the powers she'd taken, he wanted the godlight. Jessamine held the godlight, but not the powers.

"Timing and ability, I'd guess," Tomas said. "If Lachlan, Nix, and the other one came through the hedge around the same time. Maybe he didn't have time."

"But he could have incapacitated them. Locked the cottage."

"Even the gods?"

Scarlett nodded. That was true. Perhaps not, but that didn't make sense to her.

Then it hit her. She stopped short. "He doesn't know."

"Know what?" Tomas stopped a few feet away, turning when he noticed she wasn't next to him.

"That I don't have the powers. He wants them back. Not just the godlight."

"He thinks you have them."

"And maybe Jessamine is his leverage."

"Which means we will hear from him."

She nodded and started toward him. "And she will be safe, at least as long as he thinks he can control me."

Tomas

"What did you want to tell me?" Scarlett asked as they continued down the lane toward the village.

Tomas glanced at his wife ready to change the strife between them, tired of the distance.

"Tomas?" she asked, drawing him back to the lane.

"I'm sorry for hurting you," he said simply.

"Hurting me?" She sounded confused. "About my father?"

"On the table." Her breath hitched, and he glanced at her. "I didn't mean to be... rough." Only it felt like a lie. He had wanted to be rough. He wanted to be rough now.

"I wasn't hurt," she said quietly, her cheeks colored with

a sweet blush. "You didn't hurt me." Who knew his wife would blush after being together for twenty-eight years?

"But you were crying."

"I told you it wasn't that." She glanced at him and offered a wan smile. "I was just overwhelmed."

"Because of Jessamine?"

"Yes. But being with you felt like such a relief. It felt so… good, I didn't feel like I deserved it."

He hummed a sound as they walked into Sevens, pondering what she'd said. *She'd liked it.* She thought she didn't deserve to be with him. It upended what he'd always thought about how he should be with his wife, intimately. He glanced at her with curiosity but held his tongue and considered that perhaps that filtered into other areas of his life. His deference to her control had often ruled his choices, and when she'd pushed against his pushback, he'd often given way.

By the time they reached the mercantile, Tomas was even more unsettled by this realization. They checked in with Mr. Koffi, who hadn't seen Jessamine.

"Is she alright?" Mr. Koffi asked.

Scarlett exchanged a look with Tomas but then bit her lip, uncharacteristically withdrawing from the conversation. Seeing her unsure felt strange, but Tomas took charge. "No. We think she might be in danger."

Mr. Koffi's eyes grew. "What can I do?"

"Keep your ears and eyes open," Tomas said. "Anything different or strange comes through, anything said that just doesn't sit right, would you let us know?"

"Absolutely," Koffi said. "There's been so many strangers through here lately with the Queen's visit and the wedding–"

Tomas nodded.

"But yes, of course, you'll have my eyes and ears."

When they walked out into the dull gray of the afternoon, snowflakes were beginning to fall intermittently. "Should we split up?" Tomas asked.

Scarlett took his hand in hers and shook her head.

With his wife's hand in his, they stopped at the blacksmith and metalworks, the baker, and every other shop and home along the way. Tomas wasn't surprised that there hadn't been any sighting, but it felt good to know that their village community was willing to help. They finished at the Copper Pot Inn, speaking with Credence and her brother Horance.

"Have you checked in with some of the homes on the outskirts of Sevens?" Horance asked.

"Not yet," Tomas said.

"Send those soldiers Ollie... I mean, Prince Lachlan left," Credence suggested. "We'll keep our eyes and ears open here."

"Let me grab Trevis," Horance said, setting down his

drying towel on the bar. "He mentioned something about new tenants." The barkeep set down a tankard of ale for Tomas and started around the bar. "Might be a few of those along the way with all the new people up this way. And if Jessamine was taken, someone might have seen something."

"That's a good idea," Scarlett said, her eyes jumping to Tomas's as he took a sip of the ale.

A few minutes later, Trevis walked in on the heels of Horance, dusting snow from his hair. "I think it's the first true snow of the year."

"Afternoon, Trevis," Tomas said and smiled at the boy, a few years younger than Mattias.

"Sir. Horance said you're searching for Jessamine?"

"Aye," he replied. "Think she might be in some trouble. Horance here said you mentioned there are new tenants we might check with?"

"A couple. People talk about working for a few. There's Midlord Applegate over in the old Clawsen Chalet. And there's a Highlord Ramslow in the Pickering Manor. That's two I know of—the closest."

Scarlett turned to Credence. "Would you pass that message onto the two Jast soldiers?"

"I'd be happy to. Send them out as soon as it's possible to travel. How bad is that snow?" Credence asked Trevis.

"Just starting to come down."

"We should probably start home," Tomas said and

finished the ale.

"Can I give you a ride?" Trevis asked.

"No. No. We should beat it," Tomas said.

But halfway home, the light snowfall just shy of a blizzard, and they'd only worn their fall outer garments.

"Faster, Scarlett," Tomas ordered.

"My toes are frozen," she said. "We should have known better. How many years have we lived in Sevens?"

Tomas grunted. "We're almost there," he said, hopeful that was true. While he knew the road between Sevens and their cottage as well as the back of his hand, the road looked different in the snowfall. And now, without the hedge, they needed to get there before the dark set in. There weren't any lights on in the window—which he should have considered without anyone else at home.

"Maybe you should run ahead," she said. "Light the fire and the lanterns."

"I'm not leaving you," he growled. "Just move faster."

When the cottage finally came into view, the wind had picked up, and seeing the dark outline of the cottage amidst the snow felt like a miracle. Tomas grabbed hold of Scarlet, tugging her into his arms, and shuffled through the deepening snow to get her inside.

It was freezing, and both of them were wet.

"Strip," he told her. "I'll get the fire started."

By the time the fire was growing in the fireplace, Tomas

stood. "Scar?" He spun, and she stood a few feet away, dressed only in her chemise. The ivory fabric hung off her shoulder, and she shivered, her arms wrapped around her.

He held out a hand. "Come."

She took his hand and let him lead her to stand in front of the fireplace. He rubbed her arms with his hands.

Through chattering teeth, she said, "You need to get your wet clothes off."

He nodded.

She helped him remove his coat, dropping it on the floor.

"I'm sorry for not taking Trevis up on the offer of a ride," he said.

"It's okay."

He shook his head. "I know better, about snow in these woods."

She shrugged and pushed on his suspenders. "We both do. And this is a bit early."

He drew his arms through the loops and let them drape over his hips, then pulled his tunic from his trousers as she unfastened the buttons at his neck. She helped him pull it over his head.

"Your boots," she said.

He sat on the couch.

She knelt to help him.

"I can do this," he said, though his eyes greedily took in

Scarlett on her knees before him. He swallowed.

"I want to help," she said, pulling at one boot. "Let me take care of you."

He started to say he could do it but stopped.

"You have always taken care of me," she continued, removing his second boot, and setting it next to its match. She slid her hands from his ankle up his shin. "Your pants are soaked."

His heart raced at her touch, needing it more than he wanted to admit, but leaned back, his hands fisted on either side of his hips.

Still on her knees, she leaned forward and unfastened his pants with a soft touch, tugging them down. Tomas lifted his hips to help her, watching as she removed not only his outer garments but his under as well.

She folded and set the clothes in a neat pile near his boots, then studied him before walking closer on her knees so he had to spread his legs wider to accommodate her.

The light of the fire offered him the shadow of her body under her chemise, the neckline hanging to afford him the view of her bound breasts. He thought about reaching for her but didn't, his heart a cacophonous beat in his ears and vibration in his chest.

Her hands glided across the skin of his thighs.

"Scar?" he asked.

She cupped his sack in her palm and looked up at him

through her lashes. "Is this alright?"

He hesitated—not because he didn't want it but because he wanted it too much. Despite his fear that giving into what he wanted to feel with her might cloud his judgment, he nodded.

She kneaded him with her hand and leaned forward, sliding her tongue along the underside of his cock from root to tip. Having missed this intimacy with her, Tomas sucked in a harsh breath and moaned, drawing his wife's gaze before she took him into her mouth.

Scarlett

With a fervor to please him, Scarlett wrapped her mouth around Tomas's cock, and it swelled inside her mouth, stretching her as she slid down his shaft toward the base. She moaned with desire, her own wetness pooling between her legs, as she shifted her tongue to accommodate his girth, dragging it over his velvet skin, wanting this, wanting to worship him with this offering. She drew back up to his tip and released him, sliding her thumb over his head, slicking her finger with his wetness.

"You're beautiful," she murmured and licked his head.

"Scar," he groaned. "Fuck. Look at me."

She did while she took him as deep as she could into her

mouth.

His eyes were hooded, dark with desire as he watched her.

She'd been seventeen and pregnant when they'd met and just shy of her eighteenth birthday when they'd found Baba, who'd reversed the wish Tomas's parents had made. He'd been small his whole life, all twenty-two years of it by then, and had never been with a woman. Her own sexual experience had been limited. She and Tomas had learned together. They'd grown up together.

Earlier, as she'd stood in the living room of the cottage watching Tomas make her a fire, she'd realized they were alone for the first time since Jessamine had been born. Scarlett had watched him move, recalling the strength he'd shown all day as he'd talked to villagers in Sevens, thinking about him standing at the sink bare chested, considering all the ways in their lifetime together that he'd been her foundation. Remembered the dominant way he'd been with her that day and knew she needed him, wanted to serve him.

Now, she lowered her head down his shaft, taking as much of him as she could into her throat, and with her hand wrapped around his base, she used both her mouth and her hand as she drew back up to his tip. She repeated the action, deliberately slow and with pressure until he groaned with pleasure. It struck her how infrequent she'd offered her adoration to him this way—even if she felt that adoration keenly.

Tomas hissed. "Fuck." His head fell back onto the couch.

"Touch me, please," she said before driving back down his shaft.

One of his hands dove into her hair, his fingers curling and tugging at the strands. The pressure of it excited her, and she moaned and swirled her tongue on the underside of his cock, driving down on him again as her core throbbed with heat.

Tomas growled and shifted, his hips lifting from the couch, sucking in a breath as she drove down onto him again, adjusting her speed.

She wanted more. She wanted all of him.

"Fuck my mouth, Tomas," she said. "Use me." Her heart snapped hard against her chest with longing.

"Scar?"

She slid down his shaft again, looking up at him, then scraped his skin slightly with her teeth on her way up.

He hissed.

Then she stopped, her lips resting on the tip of his cock as she waited for him to take control. "Tell me what you want."

Tomas hesitated, then understanding unfurled on his features. He swore, picked her up, and flipped their positions so she was on the couch, and he stood over her.

"Open your mouth," he snapped. "Wider."

She did, one hand reaching up to grip his cock, the other grabbed one cheek of his taut ass.

"Touch yourself, Scar. Not me," he said, and with his hands holding her head, he pushed his cock into her waiting mouth, groaning as he did. "Fuck, you feel good."

She gagged at first, but breathed through it, relaxing to take all of him down her throat. He waited as she adjusted, then tested her with a gentle pulse of his hips. When she used her tongue against his skin, he pulled back, then sank into her throat, groaning as he did.

She moaned around him as he did as she asked, fucking her mouth as her eyes watered and saliva pooled. Then she reached between her legs, pressing and caressing her aching clit with her fingers like he'd told her, reaching between his legs and caressing his sacks, the skin between his sacks and his ass.

"Fuck," he shouted. "Fuck. Fuck, Scar. So good–"

His cock hardened further inside her mouth.

Her fingers slid through her slickness, bringing her close to the brink, when Tomas threw his head back with a loud groan, and fell forward, his hands gripping the back of the couch on either side of her head. "I'm coming," he grunted, and his shaft pulsed as it released his cum into her mouth.

Scarlett swallowed it, every drop, then grabbed his hip

as she released him from her mouth, licking anything left, cleaning him with her tongue. When she was done, she looked up at him.

Tomas's eyes—so dark she couldn't discern the color—watched her.

He went onto his knees before her, grabbed her hips, and yanked her to the edge of the couch. "Spread your legs, wider," he ordered.

"Tomas. I don't–"

"Hush," he commanded. "I'm doing what I want. You're doing what I want." He looked at her, waiting for her capitulation, and she gave it, needing it, spreading her legs to allow him entry.

He shoved her chemise up to her waist and tugged her undergarment down until she was bare for him. "Take it off," he said, pushing the chemise over her breasts.

She did, pulling it over her head, then removed her wrap and shivered with adrenalin, hot all over.

He grabbed a breast with one hand, while the other pushed against one of her knees, spreading her wider. The firelight illuminated the room with soft, warm light, undulating against Tomas's skin as he studied her sex.

She shivered.

"You're glistening. So fucking wet." He looked up at her face. "Did that turn you on?"

She nodded and breathed, "Yes."

Tomas swallowed, then growled as he leaned forward and closed his mouth around her clit.

She gasped. "Oh. Yes," she moaned, grabbing the back of his head, her hand sliding through his hair.

"Fuck, Scar." He let go of her breast and used his hand to press against her belly, stretching her sex. The sensation made her even more sensitive. With his other hand, he spread her wider, then, leaned forward and licked her clit, flattening his tongue, putting more pressure on that bundle that brought such pleasure.

"Oh," Scarlet cried out, rocking against his mouth.

Tomas inserted a finger inside her, then another as his tongue worked magic, growling and groaning as he did, as if she were a feast and he was a starved man. "You. Taste. Like. Heaven," he said between licks.

Already sensitive, Scarlett felt her own climax too soon. "I'm close," she gasped. "So close. Tomas. Yes." She frantically rolled her hips against his face as he fucked her with his tongue and his hands. Suddenly she was there, all the sensations gathering up into a tight knot inside her. "Please. Please," she chanted, then screamed, "I'm coming," her body exploding as everything tensed.

Tomas continued to work her through it, and though he gentled, he didn't stop.

She continued writhing and grinding against him, moaning and gasping as the orgasm lingered, unwilling to let go.

Tomas slid up from between her legs, wiping her pleasure from his face on the skin of her belly, her tits, until he leaned over and kissed her. The taste of her own pleasure grabbed hold of her insides, yanked her into the moment with him as he grabbed her legs, spreading them wider before he speared his cock into her body, driving home with one thrust.

She gasped and moaned, grabbing hold of him.

"You take it like a good girl, Scar," he said through his clenched teeth, his lips against her neck. Then he bit down, testing their connection.

Scarlett whimpered, loving every sensation rioting inside of her. From his teeth on her neck, to his skin slipping against hers, to his hips grinding against her inner thighs, to his cock spreading her wide, she was an exposed nerve, crying out with each movement. She lifted her legs, widening them even further, and pressed her heels into the back of Tomas's back. "Fuck me, Tomas," she groaned. "Harder."

He sat up and grabbed her hips, his fingertips biting into her skin, squeezing her as he fucked her.

Abruptly, he withdrew.

"No," she gasped.

But with fervor she couldn't remember from Tomas, he pulled her from the couch and flipped her onto her belly, pulled her hips up, and drove into her cunt from behind.

She cried out. "Yes. Yes."

His movement was frantic, needy, the rhythm lost as he fucked her. "Play with your clit. I want to feel you milk my cock," he growled.

Scarlett reached between her legs and touched herself, sliding through the slick around her core, feeling Tomas's cock as he drove into her again and again. As she climbed toward another orgasm, she relished every sensation, grateful for it, grateful for Tomas, needing this release to reclaim something that felt lost. She cried out. "I'm coming. I'm coming."

"I'm here," he grunted, as if he'd read her mind. But then he groaned as he tensed. "I'm here. Fucking milk me, Scar." Then he gasped, pushing into once more and stilling as his cock pulsed with his orgasm inside her.

Tomas

"Fuck," Tomas breathed, his body depleted as he held Scarlett's hips, her backside pressed tight against his pelvis, his mind whirling in the post-coital haze. He couldn't remember the last time it had been this way: frantic, needy, and so godsdamned good.

When Scarlett shuddered, then gasped, Tomas came back to himself, looked down at his wife, and noticed her shoulders shaking.

"Scar?" He pulled his softening body from her, and lifted her, turning her toward him, both of them on their knees facing one another. Concern slammed into his chest at the tracks of tears on her cheeks. He grasped her face between his hands. "What is it? Did I hurt you?"

She shook her head.

He smoothed her hair back away from her face. "What is it?"

Her watery eyes lifted to his, their gray depths an ocean of unshed tears. "I just love you so much," she whispered. "I hurt you."

His heart slammed up against the inside of his chest with cataclysmic force, and he gathered her against him. "I love you too."

"I'm so sorry for what I did."

Tomas leaned back and pressed a kiss against her cheek. When she looked down, he gently tilted her face so he could meet her gaze. "I forgive you, Scar. I will always forgive you. You are mine. I am yours. Forever."

Tears slipped from her eyes, and she offered a faint smile.

Taking the blanket draped over the couch, Tomas wrapped them together and they sat side by side, backs against the couch.

"Tell me what happened," he said.

"With?"

"Baba."

"I didn't go."

He turned his head to look at her, surprised. "You didn't?"

She shook her head and looked down at her hands.

With his fingers under her chin, he raised her eyes to his. "Tell me about the potion."

She hesitated a moment, her eyes lingering on the flames in the hearth. "I told her what I wanted to do, and she advised me against it."

"She did?" This surprised him, though his experience with Baba was limited to the one and only time he'd ever met her—the day she'd reversed his parents' wish.

Scarlett nodded. "She said I'd created a house of cards. That I should face Crue."

"Why did you discount her advice?"

She shrugged, then shook her head as if having her own internal argument.

Eventually, she turned and looked at him. "I was afraid. Afraid that he could take everything from me. You. The kids." She looked back at the fire. "The ridiculous thing is he did it without having to do anything. I did it for him." A sob caught in her throat. "Just like my father."

Tomas tightened his arms around her. "You aren't your father, Scarlett. I'm sorry I said it."

She shook her head. "No. You were right. It was awful to hear, and I might not be him, but I was acting obsessed like he was... before–" She sniffed and swiped at fresh tears, then leaned her head against his shoulder. "I'm sorry."

He squeezed her tighter against him, feeling clearer and

more cognizant of his place in the order of things for the first time in years. Everything was out in the open, the magic that had dominated their whole life together was gone, and all that remained was them and this new normal.

"We'll find her," he said, absolutely convinced that this was the truth. As much as he needed it to be true, he felt it. "We'll find him and end this."

Scarlett turned her face and looked at him, her gaze finding his.

Tomas leaned into her and pressed his lips to hers, before saying, "Together."

She turned in his arms, facing him, her eyes searching his face. Then she nodded. "You and me. Always." Then she kissed him as the first winter storm raged outside.

Tomas hadn't known he could find that inner fire again, but his body responded to his wife once more.

And for the first time since the wish had reversed, he felt at home in his body, big enough to match the size of his heart.

You can find…

In the
Shadow
of a Kiss

Novella 4.2

Brinna & Lucian

By Maci Aurora

and…

In the Shadow of a Memory

Novella 4.3

Aurielle & Nixus

By Maci Aurora

From In the Shadow of a Truth

A Collection of Fareview Fairytale Novellas
Book 4

By Maci Aurora

The Cast

in alphabetical order

Aurielle (Auri) Fareview: The fourth daughter of Scarlett and Tomas Fareview. She found an enchanted key in the Whitling Woods that trapped her in the spelled labyrinth of Nixus Uraiahs, where she was given three wishes. She fell in love with Nix and to her bewilderment, discovered they were god-yoked.

Brinna Fareview: The third daughter of Scarlett and Tomas Fareview. She is inherently good-natured and the nurturer of the family. A romantic dreamer, sometimes her dreams have seemed to come true.

Credence Crendell: Owner of the Copper Pot Inn.

Horance Forte: Brother to Credence, he helps her run the Copper Pot Inn.

Gemma Barnwell: The cook at The Copper Pot Inn.

Jessamine Fareview: The oldest daughter of Scarlett and Tomas Fareview. She is a typical oldest. A dependable and responsible daughter, she is her mother's right hand as a gifted healer in Sevens, and rarely leaves Scarlett's sight.

Johesha Malinor: The captain of the guard for the Crown Prince of Jast, Lachlan Nikolas. He is loyal, brave, and heroic. He was instrumental in saving Tarley Fareview from marauding assassins.

Keyanna Hollis: The crowned Queen of Kaloma rose to power in the male-dominated land of Kaloma. Her advisory counsel and the church of Kaloma —the Rayoran—were against her ascension and she narrowly escaped an assassination attempt on her way to negotiate a treaty with Jast—her late mother's family—for military support.

Lexa Uraiahs: Oldest sister of the twins Lucian and Nixus, she is the goddess of death and ruler of the underworld.

Lachlan Nikolas: The crown prince of Jast, he recently married Tarley Fareview. He has been tasked with remaining in Kaloma with his new wife in the capital city of New Taras to support Queen Keyanna's transition of power, a stipulation of their treaty.

Lucian (Luc) Uraiahs: Elder twin brother of Nixus Uraiahs. He is the god of light and day, but due to his meddling in his twin's life and inadvertently trapping Nix in a spell, he's been sequestered at his sky-home, Sol, until his father decides his punishment. He is the reason Auri found the enchanted key.

Mattias Fareview: The youngest child and only son of Scarlett and Tomas Fareview. At twenty, he's ready to make his way in the world.

Meera Hollis: Sister to Queen Keyanna, a Princess of Kaloma.

Nixus Uraiahs: The younger twin brother of Lucian Uraiahs, he is the god of dark and night. He fell in love with Auri Fareview when she saved him from a spell where he'd been trapped. Her sacrifice saved him and inadvertently changed the world. During their entrapment, Nix discovered he and Auri were god-yoked.

Olliander Berkman: The King of Jast's prime advisor has been sent to New Taras, Kaloma, to support Queen Keyanna's transition to power.

Ozland Aeluros: The owner of the night club Lazuli in the Lower City of Eleadia.

Poe Demertitus: Goddess of chaos and cousin to Lexa, Lucian, and Nixus, she was instrumental in trapping Nix and keeping him trapped.

making a deal with a demon to sacrifice Lucian and Nixus for power. She was spared by Auri's sacrifice, but has been imprisoned for her trickery.

Scarlett Fareview: Mother of the five Fareview children and wife to Tomas, she is a healer and extremely protective of her family. She has promised her family to share secrets she's been keeping from them.

Tarley Fareview: The second daughter of Scarlett and Tomas Fareview is fiercely independent. Considered the rebellious daughter, she is often at odds with her mother. She saved Lachlan, was asked to marry him by Queen Keyanna for the treaty with Jast, but fell in love with him. Now his wife, she is finally going to leave Sevens.

Tomas Fareview: Father of the five Fareview children and husband to Scarlett, he is the voice of reason with his wife, but also unfailingly keeps her trust by maintaining her secrets.

The Darkling: a magical creature with the ability to shapeshift, it lives on blood and will imprint on its victims, choosing either to kill immediately or satiate (turn them). A darkling has the ability to see magic spells, even those that have been designed to be concealed.

Trevis: The stable boy at the Copper Pot Inn.

The Wizard: A dark sorcerer who is looking for someone named Azleah. When he appeared at the end of In the Shadow of a Hoax, he recognized Tomas—calling him Tom—when they came face-to-face. The wizard controls the darkling.

PLAYLIST

VOW

White Lies	Sultan + Shepard, The Cut
Birdcage	Novo Amor
Sad Tune	*AK*
I See My Evil	Owsey
Autumn is Here	*AK*
Worthy	St. Finnikin
don't leave me	Desolent
STAY	Franciys
Into the Woods	Second Light
just for the night	yaeow, Rnla

KISS

Dreams in Bloom	*Sol Rising*
We Are in this Together	Ah. BLOOM, Ben Laver
Take Me Higher	yaeow, Rnla
Tender	*Aether*
Free With You	Rnla, yaeow
We Could Have it All	Emmit Fenn
Shelter	Broken Elegance

MEMORY

Trouble in Your Eyes	Yoste
Lost	Forester
Wish I Was Better	Kina, yaeow
Where I Find You	Gray North
Medicine	Boundary Run
everything to me	yaeow
Home	*Kazukii*

denotes instrumental music

AKNOWLEDGEMENTS

Well this book was a f*cking surprise! The colorful language is to denote how surprised I was. I've said from the beginning that this series was going to be four books: Aurielle, Tarley, Brinna, and Jessamine. Then all the sudden, Scarlett had to go and trap her family in a spell, Lucian and Brinna had to have their entire love story happen in a dream, and Nixus had to go and lose his memory. (What in the blazes are you doing, Maci?!?!)

As I sat down to think about Jessamine's story, I knew that I wasn't going to be able to wrap up her story without addressing some major plot points: Scarlett's past, Brinna and Lucian IRL, the magical powers, and Nixus's memory loss. These bits couldn't be done in the final book and have it about Jessamine's love story. That is when the idea of a series of novellas took shape, were written, and came to be (I wrote one for Tarley and Lachlan as well as one for Mattias, but they didn't make the cut for this publication. Maybe they'll drop in a newsletter as an extra soon).

I need to thank some fabulous people. First, Beth, who always helps me see the light when I'm lost in the dark. She is Lucian to my Nixus. Next, Stephanie, who was so supportive as a beta reader! Thank you for your feedback and help in refining these stories. Another critical person is Kate, my amazing editor. This is book number seven together and I am so grateful for your critical eye. Finally, Sara—cover artist extraordinaire—thank you so much for creating such a beautiful doorway to the stories. Your artistic vision has been perfect. I'm so grateful.

Thank you, always, to the readers who mean so much to this series. Readers like Lindsey, Joanna, Willow, Leisa, Maggie, and Mae to name a few of the original supporters when *In the Shadow of a Wish* was a new-born story. You have been champions of this series, and I'm so very grateful. Thank you to everyone who has purchased pre-orders, bought multiple copies in various formats, left a review, shared a post, made a reel, told a friend, bought a book as a gift. I'm so grateful.

Thank you to my husband, who is represented on the page in each story in some way. I love you.

Finally, my faith drives me: I am so thankful that my God, my Lord and Savior, Jesus Christ, and the Holy Spirit are my guides on this wild journey.

The Conclusion to *the* Fareview Fairytales
Publishing 2025

In the Shadow of an Obsession

By Maci Aurora

MP PRESS

Jessamine

Jessamine Fareview, first daughter of Scarlett and Tomas Fareview, was in between, trapped like a specter in her own body. For all intents and purposes, she could sense everyone believed her to be asleep, except her mind was actively awake, locked in the silent space of her body. She could hear, smell, think, and feel despite being as blind to the world as the world had been to her.

Before.

Growing up in Sevens, she'd known something was different about her, about them all, though she couldn't identify it, couldn't put words to her thoughts. To put it mildly, her mother wasn't just overprotective but overbearing. Strangely so, and more so with Jessamine than the rest of her siblings. Rarely out of her mother's sight,

Jessamine had learned the healing arts and remedies as her mother's apprentice. And she had a knack for it which had given her a sense of pride.

But there was something strange about the way others interacted with her when she went on a call. It was the way they would look at her, then look away, their eyes skimming past as if they understood she was there, but then would immediately forget.

Jessamine herself struggled to identify what made her unique, made her… well, her. She existed. She felt and loved. She interacted with her family, her sisters, others, only nothing remained to fill her and flesh her out into a wholly unique being. It was as though she were a living, breathing vessel, no more filled than that of an empty vase waiting for flowers.

She suspected it had something to do with the ribbons. Hers had always been different. Her siblings wore red ribbons at their wrists, as did she, but her crimson ribbon was twisted up with a second ribbon, a deep shimmering pink, like that of a pearl, entwined with violet threads. Beautiful, yes, but different. Just like her.

When Auri had returned from the *Great Nap Escapade* without her ribbon, and then Tarley, both with new loves, Jessamine suspected. When her mother refused to answer questions, Jessamine suspected magic was at work. But her suspicions felt locked inside her throat and even if she'd wanted to voice them, she couldn't. As if even when she'd once been awake, she'd been asleep. A living, breathing doll no more or less than the assignments she'd been given by her master—her mother.

Only something had changed—besides being imprisoned in the in-between—because the voices weren't those of her sisters or her parents.

They were strangers. Men.

All but one voice, though she couldn't place him.

Each day—she assumed, because time was strange in this in-between where she existed, moving like both the rush of a river's current but also the slow meander of a viscous, muddy mixture—he would open the box that housed her and take her hand. She couldn't see the box, of course, but she'd come to believe that to be the case, because she could hear the muted voices, hear the creak and groan of something being opened, then feel the gentle warmth of his calloused hand on hers.

Then he would whisper, "I'm here, Jessamine. I'll figure it out. I promise." In the beginning, he would tell her where they were—a manor house—in the home of a sorcerer without a name known as Master. The man with the voice that shimmered with recognition gave her the facts as he understood them. He told her she'd been taken by the sorcerer and told her he'd followed. He would tell her of the sleeping spell, the witch, the broken hedge. He would remind her of her family and that they were waiting. "I'm going to get us out of here," he'd say. "I'll get you home."

She listened to his voice, unsure who he was, only that there was something vaguely familiar about him. As he spoke, she thought of horses and the forest, of the time she'd gone after Tarley. Of the sensation of strong arms encircling her and a sturdy chest against her back. The feel of her heart's pitter patter with the movement of a horse beneath her, of a soft exhale against her neck. Of dancing and dark eyes curled slightly at the corner. She could smell leather and pine, the crispness of an outdoor chill. But time passed, somehow, and the scent of him changed to a springtime forest layered with petrichor, to the summer woods and wildflowers, to the fall forest and the depth of earthen pine, until the crispness of winter cool was on him once more.

Time was passing. She remained locked in. And the voice she longed to hear, whose touch she longed to feel never wavered, but she could hear the weariness in his sigh.

"There's a spell on the manor," he said. "Every time I leave, I forget. It is only when I return from the hunt that I remember. I don't know how to get past it."

She felt his thumb on her wrist, moving back and forth over her skin, felt a keen heat that had begun to intensify each time he touched her.

"I am failing you."

She wished she could comfort him. Wished she could lift her arm, place her hand on his, feel him with her own fingertips. Wished she could thank him for being with her. And if she could, she would assure him they'd figure it out together.

Except she couldn't. She was useless. Locked in the prison of her own body and this spell.

But she could feel his thumb, back and forth across her wrist. And suddenly it hit her.

Her ribbon was gone.

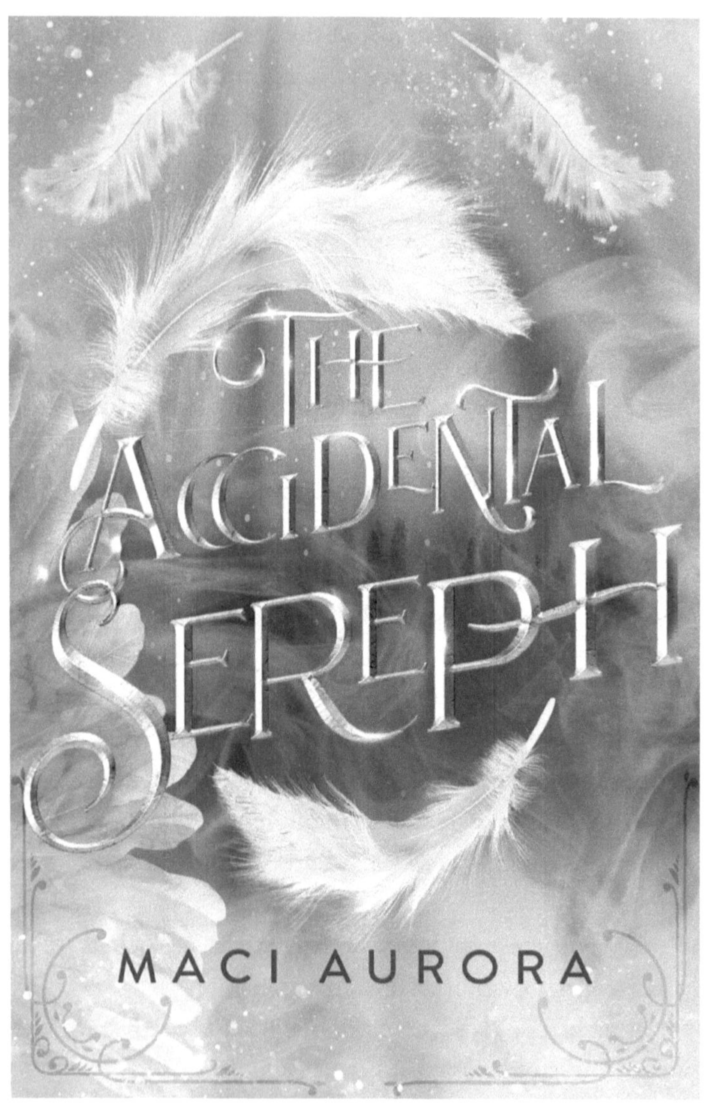
THE
ACCIDENTAL
SEREPH
MACI AURORA

ONE

Atlas

I straighten at the sound at the door of the garage. Being sure to avoid the car hood above me, I grab the blue mechanic's rag to wipe my hands and turn to watch two of my four brothers walk into the shop, their steps echoing against the concrete floor. I wait to hear how the hunt went, watching as they unbuckle and remove their leather harnesses, the weapons clanking as the metal of their knives, daggers, and other assorted weapons clash. Rome is silent but Samson hums. They're both clean, not a drop of gore anywhere.

Rome, the oldest of my brothers, hangs his harness in the cabinet, glances at me. "All good?" His intense, dark eyes bore holes into everything, including mine. His dark brows shift slightly, and that's about as much emotion as he'll offer. Fucking dipshit. But it's nearly impossible to deny Rome a thing due to that damn intensity. Fucker doesn't back down.

"Not really."

"Why not? Something happen?" I hear the concern in his voice, which sounds more like he's pissed. He might be emotionally bankrupt, but he isn't without emotions. They display in two ways: anger and angrier.

"All clear here. Chill out," I say and turn back to the car, releasing the hood so it slams back into place. "It's just being stuck here instead of hunting." My grumbling makes it seem like I'm pouting. Perhaps I am. I hate being left behind.

"Didn't miss much," Samson says as he flops onto an old red couch marred with grease stains, his gear strewn over the cushions next to him instead of put away. He leans his head back on the couch and rolls it to look at me. "A lot of nothing actually. Didn't need four of us. Didn't need two of us."

"And you're getting over an injury," Rome snaps again, over my bitterness. "You're too good a fighter. And if what the Grays have said is right, we need you healthy."

Samson makes a noise from his nose that sounds like he's annoyed. My middle brother is itching for a fight, like always.

"How did it go?" I lean against the car that occupied my hands while they are gone. I'd rather have had a bow at the ready. My four brothers might drive me crazy, but I love them. Being left behind isn't only about me, but because I worry when they're out on a job without me.

"Sammy's right. Nothing. Not a demon in sight." Rome crosses his arms over his chest and scowls, making a huffy noise of disbelief. "The question is where they're hiding. With the summer solstice coming, they're around and will show up, surely." He walks across the shop to a counter where I know he'll find something to keep himself busy. He's always busy. "Luka and Tate back?" he asks.

"Not yet," I reply. "Tate wasn't happy you didn't take him with you."

"Is Tate ever happy with any assignment?" Samson asks with a snicker.

"You're always giving Tate the shit jobs—"

"Being the youngest sucks," Samson quips.

"Checking Grams' property isn't a shit job," Rome snaps, glancing over his shoulder.

Incredulous, I tilt my head and cross my arms over my chest, "Grams could kill a demon with that razor-sharp tongue alone."

Samson laughs. "Isn't that the truth."

Rome looks annoyed—as usual. "But she'd need help if multiples show up." He pulls his phone from his pocket and glances at it. "Bus coming into the Hollow."

Samson and I groan. Buses mean tourists. Obnoxious tourists drag in the demon riffraff hiding among them, and they aren't usually the organized kind, but rather the fledgling demons or the deserters attached to the *taedae*, unsighted humans.

"Not it," Samson says.

"How's that injury?" Rome asks me.

"Not an injury," I repeat. "How many times do I have to say it?"

Rome looks me over, eyes narrowed, as if he can see beyond my skin and bones. "Fine," he relents. "You go into town. Wait for the bus to roll in, see if any demons have hitched a ride." He points at me. "But don't engage, not without backup."

I'm already walking over to the cabinet,

pulling on my harness, sliding a sharpened dagger into a sheath, along with another into my boot. "Me? Engage?" I glance at my bow but leave it, knowing I probably won't need it. Those off the bus are rarely difficult to dispatch. I glance at Rome with a smile. "Never."

Samson laughs.

I shrug into my black leather jacket and grab my helmet before I'm out the door, headed for the heart of town. After driving past Lowry's Gas and Sundries, where the bus stops, and seeing the hulking, metal can is already empty, I ride down Main. I park my bike, cross to the other side, and duck into The Hole in the Wall, a small bar sandwiched between a diner called The Getaway, and a witchy souvenir shop that sells Carran Hollow guidebooks. One of these three establishments is often the first stop for tourists, and thereby their parasitic demons, when they reach town.

My eyes adjust to the dark. There's an older guy playing guitar near the door. The shiny wooden bar is on the left and runs the length of the room. There are a few people lined up along the counter, atop barstools. Booths—mostly empty—line the right wall, and in between is a stretch of space big enough to walk between the two. I've been here before. I have been in every single shop in Carran Hollow, every single home—though the owners haven't known I was there. The Hollow is my town.

The locals glance at me then look away, giving me a wide berth. They might know me. They might know I'm a Black. If they don't, they feel it—that sensation skittering across their skin telling them danger is near. That's all that's needed.

The bartender, Gus, an older guy with a huge mustache, tops off a beer before handing it to a patron. "What can I get you, Black?"

"A shot of whiskey."

He turns to the wall of bottles behind him, selecting one and a shot glass as the bell rings, indicating someone has walked in. I glance at the newcomer since it's never a good idea to be caught unawares. Walking across the room is a woman—twenties—with a duffle slung over her shoulder. She's dressed mostly in black: black jeans with tears at the knees, and a white shirt hidden under a black V-neck sweater, also sporting holes from wear and tear. Her silver hair is shoulder-length and wavy. She's pretty— gorgeous, actually. She's got one of those heart-shaped faces with giant eyes, a pert nose, and full lips, the bottom just a touch fuller than the top. It's too dark to see the color of her eyes, but I've got a pretty good suspicion they're green, because this girl's got an aura gleaming bright green, as bright as if I were standing in front of a flashing neon sign.

My body tenses as she passes, and power hits me—the raw magnetism of it slams into mine, grips my balls before sliding up to my pelvis then racing white-hot up my spine until it hits the back of my head. I blink and grab hold of the counter to keep on my feet.

What the fuck was that?

I was born a Sentinel, have fought with all manner of creatures, fucked a few more, and I've never experienced that reaction in all my twenty-seven years.

But I have an idea.

My calix has finally arrived.

TWO

Ivy

I drop the duffle into the booth of the seedy little bar in the godforsaken fucking town where I'm stuck. I feel strange, like a bright light has erupted on my insides and filled all of them with brilliant light, then cranked up the amps so it's super loud. What the fuck? I follow my bag into the booth and rub my head, taking a deep breath, waiting for the strange sensation to wane.

It doesn't, and I don't have time to fixate on it.

I need to get the fuck out of this town.

I need a fucking map. The stupid bus broke down, and now I need to figure out a way to get another thousand miles to Onyx City. No back- up bus for another week. No rental cars. No ride shares. No train stations—unless I can figure out how to get a ride to one. The closest airport is farther than that.

Fuck.

Ignoring the tingles racing through my body, I dig my phone out of my back pocket and slide it open, pulling up the map of Murrus Province. Carran Hollow is the town where I'm fucking stuck. If I don't fucking get to Onyx—I swallow, trying not to think about it, and start looking for options.

My body heats. I can't afford to suddenly be coming down with something. I need to get to my sister.

"Hey."

I look up from my phone at the shadowy figure at the end of the table. I sigh. "Fuck off."

He—because that's a dude's voice—chuckles. "Figures," he says.

Annoyed, I use my body to deter him, but the energy pulses inside me. I shiver. Dammit. I can't be getting sick.

Fucker doesn't take a hint and slides into the

booth across from me. Only now I can see him, and I fucking hate that my breath stops up for a moment. Dear fucking fuck. He's... fuck. Not only is his voice nice, deep, with a butter-smooth accent, but he's gorgeous. His face is perfect if a bit intense and dark. Dark brows frame dark eyes with thick lashes. His nose is a touch wide and a touch crooked, from fighting, perhaps, and there's a scar across the bridge. His lips are perfectly shaped, proportional to everything on his face. There's ink sliding up his neck from under the collar of his t-shirt. All that rugged beauty is framed by wavy dark hair, short on the sides but longer on top, so strands of it fall across his face.

Fuck me, I think, but say, "What part of *fuck off* wasn't clear?" I look back at my phone but struggle to concentrate between hot as fuck dude across from me and the weird pulsing energy ripping under my skin. As much as I could sit there admiring this asshole's good looks, I don't have the time or the energy, even if I have the inclination.

He has the nerve to laugh again. "You're not from around here."

"Oh. What gave me away?"

"You look like you could use some help."

"Are these your go-to lines?" I scoff and toggle back and forth between schedules, but I blink. I can't seem to concentrate. What the fuck is wrong with me? "I suggest you return to whatever cave you crawled from and find an idiot who will fall for it."

Silence greets me. I'm used to silence, even if I hate it. It's when the voices are the loudest. The longer the silence stretches, I wonder if my words have chased him away. Disappointment slides through me considering that might be the case, because I would have liked him to work a bit harder—which is a stupid thing to think. When I look up, expecting to be disappointed, I'm not. He hasn't left. He's just sitting there in that black leather jacket with those intense dark eyes watching me, as if waiting for something.

I give him a questioning look. "What the fuck do you want?"

"Probably shouldn't say." He smirks, and fuck if that doesn't work for him. Fuck if it doesn't work for me.

Surprised by his audacity and in need of some distance, I sit back so I'm pressed up against the vinyl back of the booth. "Wow."

His grin deepens, and that fucking smile hits me right between my legs so that I have to squeeze my thighs together and adjust in my seat. That tingling sensation slams right into me, right there, as if I were touched, and I'm sure I've got a weird look. His smile widens, and it's one of those smiles that makes promises. I make a frustrated noise, which I swallow because I don't want him knowing he's got something that's working for me.

"Yeah. I mean, I should be a bit more modest, but I've heard that a few times." He leans forward, arms on the table.

I scoff and glance back at my phone, flipping between the map and the next town's schedule. "Unbelievable," I mutter.

"That too."

I can't help but look up at him again, shocked, but I want to laugh for some reason. That's even more off-putting. He's a fucking stranger in a Podunk town who could charm the pants right off me. And it's only been ten fucking minutes. In the course of my twenty-five years, I've come across my share of guys. Smart ones, dumb ones, charmers, alpha assholes, comedians, and pushovers. Some have been kind, most have not, so dealing with dudes is usually the same. But the brass on this one is something else along with... that fucking feeling that has me wanting to... I'm not sure. Moan? Vomit? Strip? Flick my clit? It's maddening.

I clamp down on my reaction, worried now as the sensation shifts, grabbing hold of the back of my neck, sending a message to the rest of me that I might need to run. Only... I don't want to run away. My impulse and the idiotic thought in my head are to run toward smirking, audacious, hottie. Which is stupid and dangerous.

It's me. I'm the stupid idiot from his cave!

"I could help." He looks at my phone.

"Did I ask?" I snap.

He leans back, and it's as if maybe I've finally pushed him off whatever track he'd been taking. He shakes his head. "Fucking hell," he mutters, "it totally fucking figures," and moves as if to leave the booth.

His words are hooks that sink in. *What the fuck does that mean,* I wonder. "I don't know you," I say.

The bell on the door jingles.

He glances at the door and tenses. "Fuck," he says under his breath, having caught sight of something that he obviously doesn't want to see. Then he glances at me, then shrugs. "Don't worry. You will." He stands, and fuck, his form is as gorgeous as the rest of him. He's long and lean. Tall in a way that isn't too much, but just fucking right. I glance at his ass as he leans toward the bar to grab something. His backside is rounded so nicely in those blue jeans that hug his hips perfectly. Not too tight but fitted enough to know that what's underneath is going to be good.

I bite my bottom lip then skim my tongue over the treatment I've given my skin.

He straightens, a helmet in his hands.

A vehicle!

"Hey," I say, scurrying from the booth before he can leave. "You've got a motorcycle." I stand, blocking him from the door.

He isn't looking at me. He's looking at

something over my shoulder. "Yeah," he says, his face tense, his demeanor completely different now.

Fuck. I might have fucked up, I think.

I glance over my shoulder at a couple of guys standing near the entrance. They look feral, red-faced, and sweaty, as if they need a fix and quick. I ignore them and turn back to hottie.

"You're right. I could use some help. The bus I was on broke down and I really need to get... somewhere else. And there's no way out of this town for another week. I need to find a ride to the nearest bus depot." I don't know what I'm doing. This is a fucking stranger, and what exactly am I suggesting? Stupid. I shake my head.

The door rings again.

I turn and glance over my shoulder. Where there were two feral, red-faced men, now there are four, and weirdly, they all kind of look the same. The second two are an amalgamation of the first two, with their ruddy features and hungry gazes.

"I'd love to talk about that ride," he says, pushing me behind him. "But maybe we can do it somewhere else."

"My bag!" I exclaim.

He leans into the booth, grabs the strap, and pulls it from the seat, hoisting it over his head and settling it on his shoulder, all the while keeping his eyes glued to the front of the room.

I want to yank my bag away from him so it's

safely back in my possession, but what was four men at the front of the bar is now eight. "What the hell?" I say, though it comes out like a whisper.

The hottie takes a step back into me, pushing me backward. "Out the back."

The mass of men at the front of the bar follows. "We'll take the calix," they all say in unison, which is creepy as fuck.

"Sorry. No can do," the audacious hottie says. "She's mine."

"What the fuck?" I snap. My first impulse is to duck around this guy for his presumptuous statement, but there's a pack of frightening- looking men between him and the door talking gibberish, and I have a horrible feeling that it has something to do with me.

Out the back.

Only he has my duffle and I need that.

"Go," he says. "As much as I would like to think I can take eight of them. It's going to be sixteen soon, and I don't like those odds."

"You have my bag. I can't leave my bag."

"I'll give it to you outside," he says between clenched teeth. "Now go."

"Listen. I don't like being told—"

"I don't give a fuck what you like right now. Get the fuck out the back," he snaps. The domineering edge of his voice snaps at my spine with something altogether pleasurable, despite the situation, and while normally I'd be telling him where he can take his bullshit, I listen, hurrying out the back of the bar. I burst through the metal door out into the alleyway, where I stumble through the door and catch myself against the pavement. When I look up, I freeze.

"What the fuck?" The words expel on a breath. I'm surrounded by a group of giant men, except they only have one eye. Then I scream.

Available Now

ABOUT THE AUTHOR

Maci Aurora has been writing stories since she was a child. At eleven, she fell in love with reading Sunfire Historical Romances about girls who made a difference in their lives while falling in love. When she discovered Lavyrle Spencer and Judith McNaught, their novels cemented her own journey to tell stories about love. Since then, she's been forever lost between the pages of a book as both a reader and a writer. While the Fareview Fairytales series is the first published under her pen name, she's written several contemporary books as CL Walters. Currently, she's busy writing the conclusion to the Fareview Fairytales series and working on some new ideas for the future. For the most up-to-date news about Maci's upcoming releases, fun extras, and behind-the-scenes bits, sign up for her newsletter on her website www.maciaurora.com.

9 7 9 8 9 8 9 1 5 4 3 9 5